CW00835627

The Lost Voyage

Titanic: The Lost Voyage

ISBN-13: 978-1654206512
ISBN: 1654206512

One

I looked at the towering smokestacks as I climbed out of the coach that had chauffeured my family and myself to the port of Southampton.

Out stepped my stepfather, Jonathan, and his servant, Mr. Webb.

My mother needed to get home so she could leave Jonathan. Webb held Mother's hand, avoiding any contact with Mother's long, flamboyant dress so as not to trip.

Jonathan snapped his fingers, motioning for Mr. Webb to bring forward our luggage from the coach.

She had never sailed, yet magazines, newspapers and people called the *Titanic* the grandest ship in the world.

"Oh! Lord! What a spectacular way to travel home, Jonathan!" Mother exclaimed.

Two months earlier, Mother had fallen ill.

"Only the best for you, Sofia," Jonathan said.

But I sensed irritation as well as aggravation in his voice.

He snapped his fingers, motioning for Mr. Webb to bring our pile of luggage forward.

"Let's move along," he said. "I can't be the last man aboard the ship."

Mother's face looked as though the color was completely drained from it.

She'd fallen gravely ill two months earlier, but my stepfather was all the more impatient about it. The owner of the Great Lakes Steel Company was going to make an entrance.

I watched Jonathan boss the *Titanic*'s bellhops around as they loaded the luggage onto White Star

Line carts.

"Be careful with that one!" he hollered.

"There are many things of great value in there. I don't want anything broken when we dock!"

"Yes, sir," the bellhop replied with a nervous smile.

Next out of the coach was the English nurse, Bella, and my sister, Katie.

At that moment, the *Titanic*'s funnels let off a gigantic boom, strong enough to cause an earthquake. Katie was startled and cupped her hands over her ears.

"It's so loud!" she cried.

She had been very cranky and disobedient ever since we arrived at Jonathan's and Mother's home in London. She quarreled with Bella, responding to all the English nurse's orders with a decisive *no*.

But today, I couldn't blame her. She was only four years old and as elegantly groomed as the grown-up women in the first class boarding area, donning her blue satin dress and shiny blue shoes. It had taken more than an hour to pin her hair against her scalp, transforming her straight red hair into curls. She looked like a much younger version of Mother, prim and proper.

Still, every time I looked at her, I pictured Bella and Mother stuffing her into petticoats to match her dress and pulling her hair while she squawked. She looked even more aggravated now, kicking and pulling at her brand new ballet-style shoes.

Mother and Bella were too strict with poor Katie. It really made me mad to see how Mother treated her only daughter. I figured that Jonathan had gotten to Mother and her sensitivity. I wasn't one bit surprised when he acted like a complete fool.

I reached out and took Katie from Bella's arms.

"Do you want to see the *Titanic*?" I asked her. "It's the biggest ship in the world."

She shook her head no.

"Come on, Katie. I bet you do," I said, as I perched her on my shoulders, knowing that she loved to sit up there. She shrieked with delight.

"Mama, look!" she said, her tiny finger pointing up toward the smokestacks.

Mother glared at me like it was a mortal sin for her only daughters to have any fun.

"Lily!" she hissed at me sharply. "You put her down on the ground right this instant and give her to Bella! Stop making a scene. And for heaven's sake and God's sake and my sake and yours and even your stepfather's, don't you dare rip her dress!"

Mother usually didn't mind if I played with Katie. But in this type of company, she expected her own daughter to look like a porcelain doll, with about the same amount of spirit. And in any event, Jonathan frowned upon us having fun. He called it "unladylike."

We hadn't even boarded yet, and Jonathan's attitude was starting to strongly influence Mother. I vowed not to let it influence me, too.

"First class passengers, proceed to the gangplanks!" a seaman bellowed, and the long line of crowded people waiting to board the *Titanic* began to move forward. We worked our way toward the gangway doors with a throng of passengers dressed in their finest outfits, butlers and maids trailing behind.

"Lily, take your ticket," Mr. Webb said scowling as he thrust it at me.

"I'm not going to hold it for you."

I knew my stepfather's servant didn't like me very much, and the feeling was mutual.

I'd hoped that Jonathan would terminate Webb's services in Kingston upon Hull and hire a new servant back in the States. Unfortunately, the crabby old man was coming to Duluth, too.

I felt a rush of relief as I stepped from the gangway to

the first class entrance of the *Titanic*.

"So long, Europe, I thought. *And good riddance."*

We were greeted by stewards and stewardesses in crisp White Star Line uniforms, who smiled pleasantly and gave a little bow.

A young woman approached us. "Welcome aboard! I'm Violet Jessop! I'm the head stewardess on the *Titanic*! Jonathan, we've anticipated your family's arrival!" the young lady said.

For a little while, I was taken aback that the crew already knew us. But then I remembered that Great Lakes Steel did business with White Star. Some of the steel in the ship's gigantic hull was purchased from Jonathan.

"Thank you," Jonathan responded in his polite but formal tone. "This is my wife, Sofia, our daughter, Katie, and this..."

Jonathan always hesitated when he introduced me because he despised me.

"This is Lily...my daughter."

"Wonderful," Violet replied as she handed Jonathan and I each a red carnation for the buttonholes in our jackets. "I will show you to your staterooms."

We followed Violet through the first class dining room, which was already set for dinner that night. Sun streaming through the portholes made the china sparkle. There were still creases in the stiff, brand-new tablecloths.

For the first time, I felt a twinge of excitement about being aboard the *Titanic*.

"The ship will be launching soon," Violet said to me as I unpacked my suitcases.

"You might want to go out on deck and see it. There's a crowd gathering on the dock to wish us bon voyage. It's quite a sight!"

I could hear Katie whining one door over. "I hate wearing this!"

I turned back to Violet. "Yes, I think I will," I replied. "And I'll take my sister."

I poked my head into the adjacent stateroom, pretending to be confused about Katie's mood.

"Katie, do you want to go out on the Boat Deck with me?" I asked. "They'll be launching the ship soon, and we can wave to all the people. It'll be fun!"

Katie's usually sad little face lit up at the mention of the word *fun*. Lord knew she hadn't had any lately, especially in London.

"Mommy, I want to go," she said.

"No, Katie," Mother replied. "It's time to rest now. Bella will fix you some tea."

"No."

"Maybe it's time for a nap, then."

"No," she insisted, kicking her shiny blue shoes. "I want to go!"

Jonathan cringed. Bella sucked in her breath, bracing herself for another tantrum.

"I'll take her," I offered again.

Mother frowned. "I don't know if it's…"

"She doesn't have to spend every minute with Bella, you know," I said. "We'll come back as soon as the ship pulls away."

"Fair enough," Jonathan replied before Mother could object. He waved his hand, as if he were eager to be rid of us.

The deck was crowded with passengers who pushed against the railing, marveling at the distance to the water. The *Titanic* had a height of more than seventy feet. Dock workers scurried around, preparing for the launch.

From our high perch, I could see where the *Titanic* sloped off to the lower decks at the stern. Another swarm of passengers had gathered there. I held Katie around the waist and settled her against the rail, where she could watch the excitement on the docks. Another long, sonorous boom echoed from the funnels.

"Lily, look!" she said, pointing. Her eyes were wide.

I tried to follow the aim of her outstretched finger. She was pointing down at the lower deck, where a single bird flew down from time to time, hovering over the tumult.

"Allie," Katie said.

She was still little enough to mix up words in ways I couldn't always understand. I thought for a moment before it dawned on me.

"Oh, yes. It's a bird," I said. "That's an *albatross*, Katie. Do you remember the albatrosses at Lincoln Park? I helped you feed them last year when we went to the park."

My mind wandered back to the big house in Duluth, on Exhibition Drive. Our street

was known around the city as "Luxury Row." The house was lonely by now. Since I'd left for London, it had been abandoned for weeks. I thought back to the day I locked it up: the rows of windows shuttered, the magnificent flower garden dead and buried under a foot of snow. That day, I didn't know when I'd be back —or if Mother ever would. Katie looked back at me with glaring hazel eyes, impatient with my stupidity. I'd seen that same look on my mother's face thousands of times… at least, before she married Jonathan.

"No," she insisted. She leaned forward to peer over the railing, so far I nearly lost my grip. "Allie."

I sighed.

"Fine then, I guess it's Allie." I'd learned not to fight these battles, especially not with a four-year-old who'd spent the morning being primped to look like a child mannequin in a department store window.

I looked over the railing at the other group of passengers. This group was far different

from the lively, overdressed first class passengers who had arrived in Southampton by private coach, burying the bellhops with mountains of luggage. Their clothing was drab.

Steerage class, I suddenly realized. They were immigrants, people coming from all walks of life, who were leaving behind their lands and their families.

Soon enough, the *Titanic*'s doors slammed shut and the gangways were sealed off. With a great whir, like the sound of a fan, the engines started for the very first time. I felt a shudder beneath my feet as the ship began to inch forward.

Two

"Here's your suite, Miss Lily," Violet said to me.

"Thank you so much, Violet," I said warmly.

"If you require additional assistance, please ring the bell by the door," she said.

"That'll be all for now, thank you," I said.

With that, Violet departed.

I remembered the first time I learned that Mother was ill.

I was at Sacred Heart Institute when there came a knock on my door.

"Come in," I said.

A young woman no older than twenty-six or so walked in.

"Miss Conkling, we've got news for you," she said.

The young woman was a Residential Assistant.

She handed me a telegram.

The address read Metropolitan Hospital.

The only city I knew that called any building or place by the name Metropolitan was London.

"It's about Mother," I said.

"Dear madam, your presence is requested at Metropolitan Hospital at the urging of your mother, Sofia Conkling," the telegram read.

I looked at her and said: "Ma'am, I must head to London. I'm not sure how long I'll be gone."

She looked at me and said: "I understand, Miss Conkling. Thank you."

With that, I took a train from Minneapolis to Chicago and rode the *20th Century Limited* to New York and boarded the RMS *Mauretania*.

I made my way from Southampton to London via another train.

I walked into Metropolitan Hospital.

A receptionist at the counter greeted me.

"Hello. I'm Jade. You must be Lily, Sofia's oldest daughter," she said.

"Yes, ma'am. Can you tell me what room she's in?" I asked.

"Certainly, ma'am," she said.

Jade walked me over to Mother's room.

"My Lily's here!" Mother said after seeing me walk in.

After Father's death, she was one of the only ones who still called me Lily.

"How are you doing, Mother?" I asked.

"I guess I'm doing okay, honey," she said.

I turned to Amelia Floyd, Mother's nurse.

"Has she had anything to eat or drink?" I asked.

"Yes, Miss Lily, but she keeps telling me that she's not feeling very well. Personally, I don't advise any transatlantic voyages by any means until she's feeling like she can handle anything," Amelia answered.

"I agree," I said.

Jonathan was having none of it.

"I have a business to run, goddamn it!" he snapped.

"I'll bring Katie's nurse along to relieve the burden on Sofia. She's been lethargic and done nothing but whine ever since we got here."

The nurse insisted. "But we haven't had a chance to determine the cause of her illness, Mr. Conkling," she said.

Jonathan rolled his eyes at her.

"Oh, please. Nothing more than mass hysteria, I suspect," he said sarcastically.

I knew exactly what people had said about Mother.

I knew that the chatter was hush-hush, quiet, behind Mother's back and at social gatherings that none of us attended.

Well, except for Jonathan, that is.

I secretly attended one and caught an earful of insults about Mother.

"Oh my God! She's too much for a man like that American steel tycoon!"

This was the chatter of couples around England and Ireland. It didn't help that they spread lies about Mother and fed the lies to their children.

It was clear that Jonathan believed these lies too.

At that gathering, I grabbed a bucket, threw up, and decided whether or not to dump it on the English and Irish or on Jonathan for lying about Mother.

All of the English and Irish societies turned out to be Jonathan's friends.

They all knew his name from the steel mills that he had in Duluth *and* in London.

In Jonathan and Mother's house in London, tensions were high.

Katie hated her dad. Who wouldn't hate a tyrant like that?

Every day for Katie was a difficult one.

She got treated very poorly at school.

Her mother wasn't feeling well.

Her father was a bastard who cared about trivial things.

The family seemed dysfunctional, to say the least.

That was when Jonathan was about.

The man was definitely not family material. He was an abusive stepfather *and* father.

He only cared about things like his not-so-great steel company and his not-so-great "friends."

To him, things couldn't be any better now that he'd suckered Mother into marrying him.

I knew that Doctor William O'Loughlin, who was the doctor on the *Titanic*, would be helpful.

The doctor was a wise and wonderful man.

"Young lady, I will look after your mother until she's better. I promise," Doctor O'Loughlin said.

"Thank you, Doctor O'Loughlin," I said.

Just then, Jonathan returned from the Smoking Room.

Of course, he was super drunk.

He went through wine and liquor like most people went through socks, peanuts, candy, fruits, vegetables, and all sorts of foods.

Doctor O'Loughlin blocked him.

"You are not allowed in to see her, sir. I am sorry, but I have strict orders that I must adhere to," he said to Jonathan.

"Oh really? And you're going to tell me that I'm not allowed to see my own wife? Get out of my way!" Jonathan roared at him.

"Sir, you're very drunk right now.

Come back later.

Perhaps when we reach New York you can see her," Doctor O'Loughlin said.

"Damn it! I'm getting in there one way or another!" Jonathan yelled.

"Sir, I'm not permitted to allow you in," Doctor O'Loughlin said.

"Fine. But I'll be back!" Jonathan said.

"Good God! That man has some nerve!" Doctor O'Loughlin thought to himself.

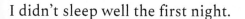

I didn't sleep well the first night.

The next morning, April 11, 1912 would have been nice if Jonathan had not married Mother to begin with.

I still dreaded that wedding.

I remembered it clearly.

Father had died a dozen years ago, but when I learned of Mother's marriage to Jonathan, I was appalled.

The marriage had occurred in the church steeple at my school, Sacred Heart Institute.

I felt like I was robbed of a decent family when Jonathan married Mother.

I knew that there wasn't much I could do about it. Well, not yet, anyhow.

Jonathan had met up with a friend of his and decided that he would join us for dinner.

"Lillian, there's someone that I would like you to meet," Jonathan said.

"I'm a little busy right now, Jonathan.

Could you wait until we're home and then I'll meet Rita Hayworth?" I asked.

"Oh my God," Jonathan thought.

A young man, with olive skin and jet-black hair stood by Jonathan. He was taller than Jonathan, but not by much.

"This is Mr. Zima, my good friend from London," Jonathan said.

"Gunther Zima, of Zima Galleries. It's a pleasure to meet you," he said, sizing me up.

"Likewise," I said, trying to keep my emotions in check.

I had heard all there was to know about Gunther Zima.

He was an art gallery owner, a rich one too, but I knew much more than that about the

thirty-year-old.

I knew that he was an art smuggler. He

trafficked in stolen goods.

The idea of such an upsetting person being onboard the ship was enough to make me want to throw up two million times.

I had been in London for 2 months now.

I'd already heard enough about Gunther to have him convicted the second he set foot on Minnesota or New York soil.

I knew that Gunther was up to no good.

But why would Jonathan become involved with such a shady character?

I had no idea. But I was determined to find out.

We were moored in Cherbourg, one of the final ports of call for the *Titanic* before heading onto New York.

As we entered the Café Parisian, I noticed Captain Smith as he walked up to us.

"I do hope that your family enjoys their stay aboard the *Titanic*, Jonathan," Captain Smith said to him.

"It's been very pleasing so far," Jonathan said.

"And I take it that this is one of your daughters?" Captain Smith asked.

"Yes, this is Lily," Jonathan said with a slight chuckle, almost like he had anticipated that Smith would ask the question.

"Lily, I see a resemblance to your mother in you," said Captain Smith.

"Thank you, Captain!" I said, smiling.

"You're very welcome. I always enjoy conversing with passengers," he replied with a smile.

Smith was known as a legendary Captain because of the many ships that he'd taken the helm on.

The ship he had been Captain of before *Titanic* was the older sister ship, *Olympic*.

On September 20, 1910, the RMS *Olympic* was involved in a collision with the HMS *Hawke* in Southampton harbor.

Although the *Olympic* was moving slowly at the time, she created enough of a suction vacuum to damage the *Hawke*.

The collision caused major damage to the hull of the *Olympic*.

The damage alone kept both the *Hawke* and the *Olympic* out of service for a little while.

The damage pushed the date of *Titanic*'s maiden voyage back almost 2 full months.

The date of the maiden voyage was effectively changed from February 20, 1912 to April 10, 1912.

It was six o'clock when we sat down to dinner.

Mother was already seated at the table with Katie and Bella.

I noticed Mother was wearing her iconic diamond necklace.

The diamond necklace owned by Sofia Conkling was the most valuable piece of jewelry in the world.

Our house on Exhibition Drive was desolate now, and the flowers wouldn't bloom until the snow completely melted, which would most likely be when we arrived back home. Our neighborhood became known as "Luxury Row."

The *Titanic*'s luxury sure beat swimming through the ocean.

God only knows what it would've been like to swim home in the North Atlantic Ocean, where the water was 4 degrees below freezing.

Friends of Mother's and Jonathan's, the McWrights, joined us.

"Oh fuck! Not her!" I thought.

It was my neighbor and archrival.

Her name was Geraldine McWright.

Mother saw me make the face that I normally made whenever I'd had it with Geraldine.

"Lily! Behave yourself and be nice!" Mother demanded.

"Hi, Geraldine," I said, trying my hardest to be nice.

"Hello, Lily," she said, listlessly.

Mrs. Wright was much more pleasant than her daughter.

"Hello, Lily," Mrs. McWright said.

"Good evening, Melanie," I said

A middle-aged man stood next to Mrs. McWright.

"Max Kellermann, Manhattan, New York," the man said as he shook my hand. "I'm the head shopper for Martin's in Brooklyn. You're the kid of that steel tycoon, right?"

"I'm his stepdaughter," I replied.

"She's at Sacred Heart Institute, but I heard the college is changing the name to the College of St. Scholastica," Jonathan said.

"Once she gets bored of attending, I'm turning the company over to her, since she'll be all set for taking care of the steel company."

Everyone at the table nodded and muttered in agreement.

I knew that Jonathan thought that my education was

nothing but a waste of money.

"I'm studying history as well as foreign affairs," I said, trying to break an otherwise awkward silence.

"Speaking of foreign affairs," Max interjected, and thankfully, steered the conversation away from me, "Mr. Zima, I have come to understand that you're a Serb."

"Only on my mother's side, yes," Gunther said.

"What's your take on the situation in Europe?" Max asked.

His vivacious New York accent made the sincere question sound almost like a farce.

"It sounds really bad."

A fierce look suddenly crossed Gunther's face.

"When Austria took Bosnia, many Serbs, including my mother's people, were killed.

It isn't something that I take lightly, and as for the Austrians. They will have hell to pay when Serbia delivers the final, crushing blow to them," Gunther answered sternly.

"I'm sorry about that," Max said apologetically.

"However, because I'm from London, I don't tend to track affairs such as those of which you speak," Gunther said in a debonair manner.

I had heard about the affair that Max had mentioned. My professors all referred to it as the "International Situation."

With the Bosnian Crisis 4 years earlier, in 1908, Austria-Hungary had seized control of Bosnia and Herzegovina from the Ottoman Empire.

I didn't really buy Gunther's claims that he didn't have any kind of underlying interest in what was going on in Serbia.

Gunther focused his attention on my mother.

"Sofia, it's my understanding that you're still recovering after your close brush with death. Please allow me to extend my best wishes to you," Gunther said.

Jonathan's face became steeled.

Mother's constrained posture slackened for about a moment or so as she tried to get comfortable in her seat.

"Thank you, Gunther," she said as she glanced at her

tea cup, not even taking the time to look up at the Serbian art dealer.

"I feel very instinctively that you're doing better?" Gunther asked.

"I'm trying to get there," Mother answered.

Gunther smirked.

"What a bastard!" I thought.

Mother was clearly in pain, so why press the issue?

It soon occurred to me that Gunther liked torturing Mother.

All of a sudden, I saw Katie push her plate away.

"I'm not hungry," she declared as she folded her arms.

"Katie, drink your tea, please," Mother said as she gently nudged the tiny saucer towards her daughter.

"What did I just say?" Katie shouted at Mother.

"All right. Then, I guess you're going back to the cabin to be with Bella," Mother said.

"No, no, no, no, no," Katie began to cry, as the other passengers glanced our direction.

Geraldine scowled.

Katie kicked her shoes against the undercarriage of the table, causing the fine china to clatter.

"Katie, be quiet!" Mother commanded, her face turning beet red as each glance started to intensify.

"I despise Bella!" Katie declared, completely ignoring Mother's attempts to calm her down. "I want Allie and only her!"

I knew that Katie was about to have another one of her world-famous tantrums.

Unfortunately for Mother, she was powerless to stop her youngest daughter.

"Katie, Allie isn't here. She left us. Remember?" Mother said, looking nervous.

"She *is* here! I *know* she is!" Katie insisted.

Now, Jonathan and Gunther both sat there speechless, forks in hand, having not said a word, but rather exchanging shocked looks.

"Who is Allie?" I asked Mother. I hadn't heard the name Allie before in my life, aside from when Katie had first mentioned her name.

"Not right now, Lily," Mother said, refusing to acknowledge my existence.

"These people didn't buy a ticket to watch Katie act like a damn circus clown!" Jonathan said.

"Fine. I'll summon Bella," Mother said rather dismissively.

I thought of everything that could possibly be whispered about Mother.

"She's unwell. She damn near had a mental break not all that long ago. Someone like her isn't fit for our social circles."

What I didn't understand, and God forbid that I should, is why Mother felt depressed about being ill.

The nurses in England already had told us that she didn't do anything to cause the illness.

I pondered the thoughts deep within my mind.

I saw that Jonathan was off to converse with others about business, and God help us all, politics.

Suddenly, somebody knocked on my door.

"Miss Conkling?" said the voice.

"Yes?" I asked.

"May I come in?" the young woman asked.

"Yes. Of course," I said.

It was Violet Jessop, our stewardess.

"Violet? What's up?" I asked.

"I've got a message for you, ma'am," said the Irish-Argentine stewardess.

"Who's the message from?" I asked.

"Your stepfather," Violet replied.

"What does that man want now?" I asked.

My mind wandered.

The last time I received any such message was when Katie's outbursts caused Mother a fit of stress.

That ultimately resulted in me coming to London.

"Your stepfather would like for you to meet him at the Squash Court, which is located on D-Deck" Violet said.

"I imagine that he didn't give you a reason why that would be?" I asked.

Violet shook her head.

"No, ma'am. I'm sorry," she said.

That's okay, Violet. I appreciate your honesty," I said.

"I suspected he wanted you to play a racquet sport with you," said Violet.

"I don't believe he's a racquet sport player," I thought.

I remembered when I was young that Father would participate in racquet sports.

He never dressed to the nines like Jonathan did whenever it was meant to be a good time.

"Thank you, Violet," I said.

"Of course, ma'am," Violet said.

I grabbed my coat and headed to the Squash Court.

"You came! It's about damn time!" Jonathan said.

"Jonathan! What is the meaning of this? Why did you want to meet me here?" I demanded.

I knew that he wasn't in the mood to play squash or racquetball.

"I can see that you're wondering why I wanted to meet you here tonight. Nobody else can know about this, but I have something to tell you," Jonathan said.

"Katie doesn't like Bella. If you need us to, we can get a different nurse for Katie when we're back in Duluth," I said.

"Lily, this has nothing to do with Katie's nurse," Jonathan said.

He looked around to make sure nobody else was watching us.

"There's nobody else here," I said.

"A sobering situation is occurring right now, and it could ruin me."

"It could ruin you too," he said, finishing his sentence.

"What is this about?

About Mother?

I understand that the nurses couldn't diagnose her illness before," I guessed.

"No. It's not about her and I prefer that you don't tell her, what with her in her condition and all.

She's unwell and mentioning this to her won't help her condition, at all!" Jonathan said.

"Fine. Tell me what I need to know," I said, knowing that I would regret it sooner or later.

"No telling your Mother. Is that clear?"

Jonathan asked me.

"Yes, sir. I understand," I said.

"A servant has stolen an important document from me.

One that could cause tremendous damage to Great Lakes Steel's standings.

When your mother, along with Katie and I, came to London, we bought a house.

Your mother tried her best to keep up with everything that I asked her to do.

But it was clear that she wasn't able to handle everything.

So, we hired a young Irish girl as a parlor maid in that house.

Two weeks ago, without any notice, she left, taking a certain letter with her.

Confidential business matters are detailed within the letter.

You realize that the very ship we're on was built using steel from the Great Lakes Steel Company, right?

The moment that the *Duluth Courant* gets hold of the letter, the steel company is doomed," Jonathan said.

"So, what you're saying is, basically, you're a marked man," I said.

"Yes. That's right," Jonathan said.

"Do you know who has the letter?" I asked.

"Because of your sister's loose lips, yes, I do know," he answered.

"Who has the letter?" I asked.

"An Irish girl. She's young, about your age. Around 18 or so," he said.

"What's this girl's name?" I asked.

"Her name is Alyson," Jonathan said.

"Or as Katie knows her, Allie," I said impulsively.

I hadn't revealed anything to Jonathan about Katie's sighting on the Boat Deck.

"In short, yes," Jonathan said.

Before I knew it, Jonathan was giving me a long-winded sob story explanation about how Allie had betrayed him and Mother.

Months earlier, Jonathan and Mother had hired Allie as a maid in their London home.

Jonathan claimed that they treated her well.

"I was her benefactor, one might say," Jonathan said.

"*Just* her benefactor?" I asked.

"I guess I deserve that," he said.

"You're lucky she's onboard," I said.

"You could say that. Needless to say, I checked with the Purser.

She was scheduled to sail on the *Philadelphia*, but those passengers were transferred aboard the *Titanic* due to a coal strike," he replied.

"They're coming in waves, flocks, whatever you want to call it."

He was right. I knew that there were Irishmen working in Jonathan's steel mills both in Duluth and London. I'd seen them whenever I visited the mills. They lived in a tenement housing community called Irishtown. Compared to

Duluth, the place looked like Harlan County, Kentucky. A real dump. The town was littered with whiskey bottles and beer bottles and beer cans. It was a very unpleasant place.

"I can't accost her myself," Jonathan continued. "It's too dangerous for me, a powerful business owner, to be lurking around third class. You're still in your teens. You can get into third class undetected."

"I'm not going to sidle into steerage.

Why don't you get Webb to do your dirty work?

These are the kinds of things the guy lives for!" I said, astonished by the force of my voice.

"God damn it, Lillian! Listen to what I'm saying! I have endowed you with everything that my father and myself built, with effortlessness on your part. As you explore the ship, look around you and take in your surroundings!" he said.

"What would you stand to gain if Great Lakes Steel were to be shut down? The documents are crucial for myself and for you," he continued.

"What do you need me to do?" I asked, regretting it the minute the words came out of my mouth.

"Find her. The Third-Class passengers tend to gather every night in the steerage lounge.

It's the lone place they can socialize because the men's cabins are towards the bow and women's cabins are towards the stern. I want to know how much money she requires to turn over the letter to me. Once you have a set price, I'll summon Webb to make the exchange," he answered.

"Do you really think this is the best idea?" I asked.

"Ah, don't be scared of her. It's not like I plan to send you into the bear's den without any backup," he said.

Jonathan looked around again, making sure that we truly were alone. After assuring that we were alone, he reached into the pocket of his jacket. He pulled out a gun and gave it to me.

"The last thing we need is a scandal. Do this to save your mother the humiliation of such an event. It's the least you can do for everything the poor woman's been through," he grumbled.

"If anything goes wrong, use that gun."

"I won't let you down, Jonathan. Your instructions were very clear," I said, nodding.

"Good girl. Now, if you'll excuse, I'm off to meet Gunther in the Smoking Room. I'll talk to you more about this tomorrow. And not a single word of it goes through to your mother. Understood?" Jonathan asked.

"Crystal clear, sir," I said.

I left the Squash Court quiet as a mouse.

I tried to control the thoughts that raced through my mind at over 20,000 miles a minute. Every waking moment was pure agony.

"What the hell was Jonathan doing on the European side of the Atlantic while I was at Sacred Heart Institute?"

"How the hell did he know about the school's name change when I hadn't even revealed it to Mother?"

"What was really going on with Mother? Why couldn't anyone diagnose her?"

These burning questions inhabited my mind.

"Bit of a rough night?" I heard someone ask.

I spun around to see Max Kellermann as he stood behind me, exhibiting his usual jaunty smile.

"Is it really that obvious?" I asked.

"Yep. I can read ya like a book," he answered me.

"Oh, God. I need to do better at masking it," I said.

"Lily, how are you when it comes to playing cards?" Max asked.

"Are you challenging me to a game of Blackjack, Max?" I asked.

"Sheesh. That obvious, huh?" he asked.

"Well, when it's the only card game I know how to play, then, yeah," I said.

"I know that normally girls and women aren't allowed in the Smoking Room, but there's a game about to go on up there and there's a guy that really wants to meet ya," said Max.

"What's the guy's name?" I asked.

"François," Max replied.

"All right. Let's go," I said.

 Max walked me up to the Smoking Room.

"Everyone, I want you to meet my friend, Lily Conkling. She's Jonathan Conkling's stepdaughter. You probably already know about Great Lakes Steel Company," Max announced, introducing me.

"Ah. So you are the famous Lily Conkling. Your mother owns the most valuable necklace in the world," François said.

"*How does he know?*" I wondered.

"You appear to have done your research on me,

François," I replied.

"What do you say to Blackjack?" he asked me with an accent thicker than the snow in Minnesota.

"Heh. Bring it on, hotshot!" I said.

"Very well, mon ami," he said.

One of the onlookers turned to Max.

"You think this girl's as good at this as she says she is?" the onlooker asked.

"If I know Lily, she'll be able to pull off anything," Max answered.

I looked at my hand.

"Hmm. A 9 and a 2. Well, that makes 11," I thought.

"Hit me," I said.

François passed me another card.

I now had 3 cards.

"Hmm. 9 plus 2 is 11. Plus 10 equals... 21!" I thought cheerfully.

"I think I'll stand," I said.

"Well, it looks like you've bested me, madam," François said, gracefully accepting his defeat.

"Lily beat François at his own game!" another onlooker said.

"You know it! Hey, barkeep! Pass me a cold one, would ya?" Max requested.

"Of course, sir!" the bartender said.

"Until now, I had my doubts that anyone could hold their own against François Fournier," said another.

"You play with such grace, François," I said.

"Why, thank you, mon ami," he said.

"So, how did you know about my mother's necklace?" I inquired.

"Ah. It is a pitiful thing, this burden that I carry around knowing events before someone can ask me how I know such things. But, when you're playing cards, you tend to learn something," François replied.

"You mean you're a psychic?" I asked.

"Yes. In a manner of speaking," he answered.

"Well, can you tell me my future?" I asked, jokingly.

François laughed.

"Mon ami, I cannot tell you what the future holds for you, but I can tell you what the future holds for the *Titanic*," he said in reply.

"What *does* the future hold for the *Titanic*?" I asked him.

"Take heed of this warning. For you shall know that on Sunday night, April 14, chaos will ensue. A great tragedy is coming. Yes. A very great tragedy indeed. I see something massive in the path of the *Titanic*. It looks like something made of..." François said as he cut himself off. He let the words sink in.

"What? What does it look like?" I asked, knowing I would regret it immediately.

"Ice," François finally said, finishing his sentence.

I turned to Max.

"Max, I hate to be the one to ask you to do this, but can you go find Captain Smith?" I requested.

"Yes, I can," Max responded.

"Thank you, Max," I said.

"Not a problem," he told me.

It wasn't going to be too long before we were to meet with destiny, with fate, and the Lord, our

God would soon put us to the ultimate test of survival.

But, for now, I had a mission to complete.

I had to get the letter back from Alyson.

I hadn't had much time to think of what I was going to say to her.

"What the hell was I supposed to say? Hello. My

name is Lily Conkling, and because of your recklessness, you've put my inheritance in jeopardy?"

I couldn't help but wonder.

"Is this Alyson girl really worth all the trouble?"

"Why send me?"

To me, it seemed like Jonathan was simply worried about himself and his damn steel company.

However, the luxury of the *Titanic* relieved my qualms.

I felt bad for Alyson.

She was an impoverished young Irishwoman.

Jonathan had made such wild allegations against the young lady that I didn't know whether to trust him or not.

Alyson was also in possession of a very rare book.

It was called *The Rubaiyat of Omar Khayyam.*

I couldn't afford to procrastinate anymore.

I had to find Alyson.

Three

I headed to the lift just off the Forward Grand Staircase on B-Deck.

"Evening! I'm the lift attendant and you'll not find one better than me where you need to go! Where to?" a young man with blond hair asked me.

"I'm on my way to meet someone," I said.

I couldn't reveal the fact that I was headed to Third Class.

"Ah! And who might you be meeting with tonight?" the attendant queried.

I was backed into a corner. I had to admit it.

"I'm supposed to be meeting with a girl in Third-Class," I admitted.

"Ah. Shantytowning, are we, lassie?" he asked.

"Yes sir," I answered.

Shantytowning, also known as slumming, was frowned upon by White Star. First-Class passengers were rich and steerage passengers were dirt poor.

"Ah. Very well, then. Take my lift to D-Deck. Find the Reception Stairs for Scotland Road. Then go down the stairs to reach Steerage," he said.

"Thank you very kindly, good sir," I replied.

"Where do you feel like going?" he asked inquisitively.

"Please take me to Scotland Road," I said.

"Very well. Mind the gate!" he replied.

I knew that it was going to be very rowdy in the Third-Class Lounge.

But I didn't expect it to be a raging party.

"Hello?" I said.

"Oh! 'Ello there! What can I help ya with tonight?" a young Irishwoman asked me.

"I'm looking for Alyson," I said.

"You mean *that* Alyson?" the young lady asked.

I turned and looked.

A young lady with long flowing red hair came into focus.

I approached her.

"Hello. You must be Alyson," I said.

"Hello. Yes. I'm Alyson," she said.

"I'm Lily. Pleased to meet you," I said.

"What can I do for you, Lily?" Alyson asked.

"Tell me how much you want for the return of the document, Allie. Please?" I begged.

Allie sighed.

"5,000 dollars," she said.

"Fine. Let me talk to Jonathan about it," I said.

"If you don't get me 5,000 dollars by Tuesday, this letter *will* go to the press once we arrive in New York," Allie replied.

"I already know about the contents of the letter, Allie. The $5000 price tag doesn't scare me," I said.

"You're either crazy, brave, stupid, or all three, Lily," she said in an almost icy tone.

"I'm very brave. Hell, I'm as daring as I need to be whenever it's necessary," I said in reply.

I rushed out of Third Class and headed to the Grand Staircase.

"*Goddamn it all! I can't keep up this bullshit assignment!*" I thought.

I had to find Jonathan.

I retired to my room for the evening.

Four

The next morning, I decided to walk along the deck of the *Titanic*.

"Rough night last night?" I heard a man ask.

I whipped around and saw Max Kellermann standing behind me.

"Yeah. I guess you could say that," I answered.

"Because of Jonathan and his insanity?" Max asked.

"Yeah. But how did--" I began.

"How did I know that it was because of Jonathan?" Max asked.

"Yes. I hadn't even told you about the assignment that Jonathan had given me," I answered.

"Well, I know how much you despise him. Hell, I hate the son-of-a-bitch, too," Max replied.

"I swear to God. I don't know why he wants me to retrieve some stupid letter," I muttered.

"Whoa! Whoa! Whoa! Whoa! Whoa! Whoa! Back up a second!" Max said.

"What is it, Max?" I asked.

"The letter you're talkin' about," Max answered.

"Yes?" I asked.

"Can you tell me what's so important about getting it back?" Max inquired.

"Oh. Nothing really. Just that it's a confidential document that could spell the Great Lakes Steel Company's demise, that's all," I said in reply.

"Sounds like the mill's been makin' bad steel, if ya ask me. That could spell bankruptcy or even some other bad things for sure," Max replied.

I knew exactly what Max meant when he said "some other bad things for sure."

Investigations, blackmail, extortion, not to mention even the most unthinkable crime of all: murder. These were just some of the things that were possible.

"I know how much you and I both hate Jonathan, but I think I better warn him," I said.

"Okay," Max responded.

"I'll catch up with ya later, Max," I said.

"Right. Sounds good," he called out to me as I walked away.

I headed to find Jonathan.

I walked through the First-Class Lounge to the Aft Grand Staircase, admiring everything, but still fully aware of the psychic reading that François had made earlier on during the voyage.

"What if he's right? What if something really is going to happen to the ship?" I wondered.

The thoughts bothered me to no end.

"I have to find Jonathan," I thought.

I knew what my main priority was.

I had to inform Jonathan.

Jonathan and Gunther were sitting in the Smoking Room.

I walked in.

"Sorry to disturb you both on such a fine morning, gentlemen," I said, rather calmly.

"What is it?" Jonathan asked, in a manner that was rather blunt.

"Jonathan, I spoke to Allie last night. She wants $5000 for the return of the letter. Also, I ran into Max Kellermann this morning on the deck. He confirmed what I already knew, sadly. Sir, your mills have been producing bad steel. Why wouldn't you tell me this when we first met in the Squash Court?" I asked, breaking the bad news.

"It was for your own safety, Lily.

You see, when my father started the Great Lakes Steel Company, the steel only had to be heated to somewhere between 1200 and 1400 degrees. In this day and age, the steel must be heated to 1500 degrees. The rivets were heated to the temperatures used back when my father founded the company," Jonathan answered.

"You're a fucking idiot! Do you realize what kind of fucking danger you've put us all in?" I snapped.

"Whoa! What do you mean when you say danger?" Jonathan asked.

Oh please! Don't act all innocent! You're a bigger threat to the world than you led me to believe!" I said.

"How so?" Jonathan asked.

"Oh, I don't know. How about by producing bad steel?!" I answered angrily.

"You don't care about anyone but Gunther and

yourself! You're a danger to society!"

"Settle down!" Jonathan told me.

"I will not calm down! How could you be so twisted?!" I demanded.

"It's an honest mistake, Lily," Jonathan said.

"Hmm. Why don't I believe you?" I asked.

"Maybe because you've always hated me?" Jonathan replied.

It was meant to be a rhetorical question, but he was right.

The fact that he knew that much made me even

more alert.

There was definitely something off about him.

That was the real reason that I couldn't trust him.

Jonathan was hiding something more than just a letter about bad steel.

But *what*?

What was he hiding?

I didn't know what to expect.

Jonathan. The man who ran the Great Lakes Steel Company.
Was he being honest or was he feeding me a

line? Blowing smoke?

I retired to my stateroom for the night and went to sleep.

Five

The next morning, I headed out on deck for a walk again.

It had become my daily routine while onboard the *Titanic*.

I kept pondering the very thoughts that had eaten away at my brain the night before.

"How can I be sure that he's not playing me for a fool?" I wondered.

It wasn't until I met up with Max that I would meet someone else too.

His name was Heinrich Helmfried. He was a student at the University of Nuremberg.

It wouldn't be until later on that day that I learned the truth about him.

It came at a moment that I never expected.

As I sat down to lunch with Max, Heinrich sat down next to us.

Heinrich made a very unusual suggestion.

"Lily, why don't we take this to your stateroom?" he asked.

"It'll be much quieter there and I can tell you both what you need to know about me."

I turned and looked at Max.

"Well, Max?" I asked.

"Sure. Why not?" Max responded.

We headed back to my stateroom.

The mystery that surrounded Heinrich was greater than anything either Max or myself could have imagined.

We sat down at the table.

Heinrich sat quietly and intensely for a few moments.

"What I am about to tell you must be kept between only the three of us," Heinrich said.

"Of course, Heinrich," I said.

"Okay. I'm a student at the University of Nuremberg. However, that's a mere cover story," Heinrich said.

"The only kind of person who would need a cover story is a…" I began.

"A what, Lily?" Heinrich asked.

"A spy," I said.

"You're correct, Lily," Heinrich said. "The truth is I *am* a spy. I'm an agent for the Okhrana, the Russian secret police."

"Then I'm sure you're aware of the big scandal," I said, not naming Jonathan or Gunther personally.

"The scandal about the steel and the fact that your stepfather is working with the most dangerous man on the Atlantic Ocean?" Heinrich asked. "How could I *not* know?"

It soon became clear to me that he was obviously keeping up with major news events.

But another thing bothered me. *How* exactly did he know about the steel? I hadn't mentioned it to him.

The problem was greater than I had been led to believe.

"Heinrich, is there anything else that I should know about?" I asked.

"Yes Lily, there is one more thing that I'll tell you right now," he answered.

"What is it?" I asked, rather nervously.

Heinrich could sense the tension in my voice.

"What I'm about to tell you could put my whole career on the line. But I think you should know the truth, anyhow," he replied.

I thought for a moment.

"*I should know the truth? About what?*" I wondered.

Suddenly, I gasped.

"It's about Gunther and Jonathan, isn't it?" I asked.

"Yes. Unfortunately, it is," Heinrich answered.

"What is it that you're going to reveal to me?" I asked.

"Gunther Zima is a militant for Unification or Death, but you may know this organization of terrorists as The Black Hand," Heinrich answered.

"And what about Jonathan?" I asked.

"Your stepfather is a thief. A con artist. A scammer," Heinrich said to me.

"So, all of those things about him being some reputable metallurgist were lies?" I asked.

"Yes. And that's not all. You see, I have been watching both men very closely. Jonathan frequents expensive materials," Heinrich said.

"When you say he "frequents" expensive materials, what exactly do you mean?" I asked him directly.

"I mean he smuggles such objects. I'm talking about items like diamond necklaces, rare books, paintings, and more," Heinrich said.

"How do I know if he smuggled something onboard?" I asked Heinrich.

"You wouldn't be able to tell just by looking at it. In order for the scheme to work, a copy must be made of either a necklace, a rare book, or a painting. The problem with fakes popping up is that you'd have to look extremely close at the object in question. That's how a con artist operates best, Lily," Heinrich answered me.

"But what would I have to look for in order to ascertain that it *is* a fake and not the real item?" I asked.

"Look for flaws. Imperfections. Poorly written prose. Uneven brush strokes. Canvas that's been put through a distressing process to make it look aged. Merry-Joseph Blondel created a painting that was worth hundreds of thousands of dollars. It was called La Circassienne au Bain," Heinrich said in reply.

"Is there a specific item that you seek, Heinrich?" I asked.

"Yes. It is a notebook. A very important notebook," he answered.

"What does it contain?" I asked, my curiosity having piqued.

"Names of Russian revolutionaries living in exile. They're called Communists.

They oppose the Czar. They're also called Bolsheviks.

If they were to overthrow the Romanov Dynasty, there would be chaos and hell in Russia.

It could spell the end of a civilized country," he replied.

"But, if we get our hands on that notebook, we

could send it to the Okhrana, right?" I asked.

"Yes," Heinrich said.

I sensed that he had a question.

"But?" I asked.

"But what?" Heinrich asked.

"I know you're wondering about something," I said.

"But how will you obtain that notebook without getting caught?" Heinrich asked.

"Leave it to me. You said that you need a specific notebook, right?" I asked.

"That's right. It should have a picture of a black hand drawn on it," Heinrich said.

"Thanks. I won't be very long," I said.

"Lily! Wait!" Heinrich said.

"Huh?" I asked.

"What in God's name do you think you're doing?" Heinrich asked.

"Getting the notebook for you," I said.

"You can't just walk into the room and grab the fucking thing!" Heinrich said.

"Why not?" I asked.

"You need some form of security!" Heinrich said.

"What kind of security? A gun?" I asked.

"What do I look like, an assassin?" Heinrich asked.

"Just wondering," I said.

"Here. Take this," Heinrich said to me. He handed me a pen.

"A pen? How the hell is a pen going to stop anyone?" I asked.

"It may look like an ordinary pen, but this isn't your everyday pen. Not even close. This pen releases a burst of knock-out gas when activated," Heinrich said.

"Thanks! I don't suppose you have a few more like this, do you, Heinrich?" I asked.

"I'm not sure, but I can look," he answered.

"Okay. Thanks. While you look, I'll go take care of the notebook," I said.

"Okay," Heinrich replied.

Six

I made my way to Gunther's stateroom.

I had remembered what Heinrich had said.

"Jonathan frequents expensive materials. He smuggles them."

"Not anymore," I thought.

"If I got caught, how would I get out of the situation?" I wondered.

I thought for a little while longer.

"A lost contact lens," I finally thought.

I walked into the stateroom.

"He's not back yet," I thought.

On the dresser, there was a Matryoshka doll.

I noticed the combination lock.

"Damn it! A tumbler lock!" I thought.

I was about to give up hope when all of a sudden, I noticed odd numbers on each side of the doll.

I spun the dials and opened the safe.

I grabbed the necklace.

I put it back together and then reset the combination.

I saw a notebook lying on the table.

It had a drawing of a hand in black ink on it.

I grabbed both items and headed out of the room.

I kept thinking about Mother.

I had to check on her and warn her about Jonathan.

I headed to Jonathan and Mother's room.

Violet Jessop, our stewardess for the voyage, had made tea already for Mother.

Mother's ashen face all but sagged.

I had to tell her.

"Lily, is that you?" she asked.

"I'm here, Ma," I said.

"Thank God for Bella," I thought.

Katie's quick thinking had actually saved Mother.

When Katie noticed she was short of breath, she summoned Bella immediately.

Bella immediately summoned Violet.

Violet was kind as could be.

"It'll be all right, Mrs. Conkling," she said.

I looked at her.

She looked back at me.

"Violet, may I speak to you in private?" I asked.

"Lily, if you want to speak, you don't have to ask. You can just make some sort of motion for me to go with you and I'll gladly do that," Violet said.

We walked out of the cabin for a little while.

"Miss Jessop, I need to know. How is my mother doing?" I asked.

"Well, she's starting to improve a little bit, but I have a feeling that someone in your family is not at all who they claim to be," Violet answered honestly.

I looked down and sighed.

"I know. And I know exactly who and I know exactly what the crime is that's been committed," I said.

"A crime? What do you mean, Lily?" Violet asked.

"I mean that Jonathan, the man whose steel built this great ocean liner, has been poisoning my mother. Of course, I have to prove it, but I know that it's happening and I can't let him get away with it any longer!" I answered.

"What kind of evidence do you have so far?" Violet asked.

"None, except for the word of a young man that I met earlier," I said.

Violet looked worriedly at me.

Lily, it's not safe to go about this alone," Violet said.

"I understand, Violet," I said.

"So, let me help you out," Violet replied.

"Okay. Let's go," I said.

"But before we go, here. Take this."

I handed her the gun.

"Jesus bloody Christ! What do you have this thing for?" Violet asked.

"Jonathan gave me that gun and thought I would need it," I admitted.

"Well, I'll hold on to it for you. For now," Violet replied.

"I can't let you use it unless you absolutely need to use it."

"There's one more problem, Violet. Jonathan's with an accomplice," I said.

"You mean that sleazebag art dealer?" Violet asked.

"What the—? How did you know?" I asked.

"I'm not just a stewardess and nurse, you know. I'm actually undercover," Violet answered.

"I'm an agent with the British government. I had been aware of Mr. Conkling's corruption and his misdeeds from the start. I didn't want to blow my cover. But now, I need concrete evidence."

I nodded.

Seven

We headed to the First-Class Lounge.

We needed to conceal ourselves, yet still be able to hear the conversation between the most wanted men in the world.

I found a great spot to hide with Violet.

Jonathan was with Gunther, alright, but they weren't planning to stay in the Lounge.

If I knew Jonathan like I thought I did, he and Gunther were going to be bringing Webb into the scheme and cutting me out. We made our way to Mr. Webb's cabin.

We got close enough to the door to hear what was being said.

"Ah, Mr. Webb. How kind of you to join us. I'm

glad you're here. You see, Gunther and I believe that there's a traitor among us. Don't look so startled. It is not you," Jonathan began.

"You mean… Lily?" Webb asked.

"Lillian has hated me since the day I married her mother. And, I've hated her ever since. Kaitlyn was the only legitimate child I had with Sofia. I thought Lily would come around, act like she gives a damn about the business. But no," Jonathan said as he lit up a cigarette.

Jonathan was the only person who called Katie by her full first name rather than her nickname.

"It appears that Lillian has been enjoying her visits to steerage. I might keep her on long enough to retrieve that letter," Jonathan said.

"You don't have it yet?" Webb asked.

"You really expect me to pay $5,000 for the damn thing?! I would kill to get that information back!" Jonathan said.

"Your plan to get your wife committed backfired," Webb said.

"Don't you dare bring that up. I know I failed once. But, my second plan…" Jonathan said as he paused.

"Yes. Of course. The thallium was enough to cause epileptic episodes," Gunther reminded him.

Jonathan laughed.   "I think everyone believes now that she's mentally unstable."

"I've heard all I need to hear," Violet said to me, softly.

"Great. So, how do we go about this?" I asked her in a whisper.

"It won't be easy," Violet said.

"I know," I said.

"It's going to require precision and tenacity. I hate to ask you to do this, but I need someone to bait these men into a trap. Can you do that?" Violet asked.

"Yes. But, it would help to know exactly how you plan to trap them," I said.

"It's going to require the usage of the Cargo Hold," Violet said.

"The Cargo Hold? Why in God's name do you need that?" I asked.

"Well, it's either that or we take them up to the Boat Deck and toss them overboard," Violet answered.

"I prefer putting them in the Turbine Room," I said.

"Good God! You're dark!" Violet said.

"Well, tossing them overboard didn't seem like a great option and the Cargo Hold has too many valuables," I stated.

"You want them to mess around with the turbines and possibly cause damage?" Violet asked.

"If we don't find some way to contain those men, we'll never be able to get off this ship alive!" I said.

"Tell me something I *don't* know!" Violet replied.

"Okay. We're all doomed," I said.

"That's not funny, Lily," Violet replied.

"I was being serious, Violet," I said.

"Oh. How exactly are we doomed?" Violet asked.

"You can't let anyone else know that I did this, Violet. Please understand," I said.

"Okay. Then tell me, Lily. It's okay," Violet said.

"I played cards in the Smoking Room with some Frenchman. Apparently, he can see the future. He warned me of a block of ice. The *Titanic* is in great danger and all who are aboard her are also in very grave danger. Heed this warning. Tell only who you must about the ice," I said.

"You mean Fournier? That guy who gossips about others and their lives?" Violet asked.

"So, you know him? He was an interesting man to speak to when I beat him at his own game," I said.

"If Jonathan finds out that I was in the Smoking Room, he'll kill me."

"Lily, settle down. I'm glad you told me. You did the right thing by telling me. Everything that you tell me is confidential. Your stepfather doesn't know the half of what Heinrich and myself do. If your stepfather ever truly knew, he would have hunted both of us down a long time ago. I wouldn't be able to speak to you if my cover had been blown," Violet replied.

I knew that I could trust Violet. Thank God for her. I *had* to tell her the truth about Jonathan.

"Violet?" I asked.

"Yes, Lily?" Violet answered.

"There's something I've been holding back on telling you. I thought I could trust myself to keep this information as well concealed as possible, but I need to admit this," I said.

"What is it?" Violet asked.

"Jonathan had purchased a diamond necklace for my mother, then had a fake one made, stole the real one, put it in Gunther's cabin in the safe, told my mother he'd left it with the Purser, then gave her the fake one. He also had given his former maid a rare book," I said.

"Rare book? What rare book?" Violet asked herself.

"It was a jewel-encrusted book," I said.

"Oh. I know the book you're talking about!" Violet replied.

"You do?" I asked.

"Of course! It's called *The Rubaiyat of Omar Khayyam*," Violet responded.

I knew that I had to reel Jonathan in somehow.

"Violet, I have a plan to capture Jonathan, Gunther, and Webb. But, I'll need your help. Are you in?" I asked.

"Of course I'm in, Lily. I wish that we didn't have to use live bait in order to capture them," Violet answered.

"Thank you, Violet. I really appreciate your help," I said.

"What's the name of the Irishwoman?" Violet asked.

"Alyson," I answered.

"Or Allie for short?" Violet asked.

"Yes," I replied.

I knew it wouldn't be long before Jonathan, Gunther, and Webb tracked me down.

I also knew that Violet was ready to jump on them.

However, I wondered about something.

"How good of a shot was Violet?"

I tapped her on the shoulder.

"What is it, Lily?" Violet asked.

"Who should we warn first?" I asked.

"Warn your mother, your sister, and Bella. I'll handle Alyson," Violet said.

"Got it," I said.

Violet and I split up.

Violet made her way to F-Deck.

I made my way to Mother's cabin.

I burst through the door.

"Mother! Are you okay?" I asked.

She sat up calmly and said: "Yes, Lily. I'm fine."

"Okay, well, I have something to tell you," I said.

"What is it?" she asked.

"I wish I had an easier way to tell you this, but I know who's causing your illnesses and what he's using to do it," I answered.

"Who's causing this and what is being used and why?" she asked.

"It's Jonathan. He's poisoning you and it's all to commit you to a sanitarium," I said.

"I had my reservations about him when we first boarded," she replied.

"Then, why didn't you admit that you were having second thoughts about your marriage to him?" I asked.

"I see now that my marriage to him was a mistake. A very stupid mistake. He's friends with a German who's part of some organization called ——" she said, struggling to think of the name of the organization.

"The Black Hand," I said.

I dug into the bureau and pulled out a black belt.

Just then, Jonathan walked in.

"What the hell do you think you're doing in here? Get the hell out of my bureau!" he shouted at me.

"I was just looking for a belt," I lied.

"Well, I'll say. Looks like you found one," he said.

The belt wasn't like the ones that we normally wear. It wasn't a belt with a quick snap in the front.

"Actually, I think I better look around my room," I said.

"Yes. You probably should. I'll see you at dinner," Jonathan said to me in an icy manner.

I headed back to my cabin.

The night had not gone as I had planned so far.

While I was in my cabin, I grabbed my favorite belt.

It snapped over my dress in the front very easily.

I headed for the First-Class Reception.

While our families were distracted, Geraldine, who I normally didn't get along with, gently pulled me aside.

"Quickly, Lily. I don't have much time," Geraldine said. She held in her fist a piece of paper with something scribbled on it.

"It's from Heinrich," she said.

"*Meet me in the Gymnasium tonight at 11:30. Tell only who you must*," the note read.

"The Gymnasium? Why there? I'm not going to be exercising this late night," I said.

"I highly doubt that's why he wants to meet you there," Geraldine said.

She made a subtle motion towards Jonathan.

"Nice thinking!" I said. "Geraldine, how does Heinrich about Jonathan's activities when I didn't even know about them to begin with?"

She shrugged.

"I don't know. Heinrich is a very interesting man. Very enigmatic. He wouldn't tell me much. He only told me that you must meet him before we arrive in New York. He said to me that time is at a premium," she said.

I knew that something was amiss.

Suddenly, the tough demeanor that Geraldine normally expressed was completely gone.

"Is your family in trouble, Lily?" Geraldine asked worriedly.

"I don't know. I honest to God hope not," I said. In essence, I slid the note into my pocket.

If my family *was* in trouble, there were only three people who could cause it, but they had to work together to make it happen.

Eight

We approached the table.

"Wait a second!" Geraldine exclaimed.

"What is it?" I asked.

"Let's sit at a table away from our families," she suggested.

As night fell on April thirteenth, I knew that I had no choice but to tell Geraldine the sobering truth.

"Geraldine?" I said inquisitively.

"Yes, Lily?" she asked.

"I-I-I-I, I have something to tell you," I stammered.

Geraldine looked into my deep blue eyes and said: "Please tell me, Lily."

"Let's meet back in my stateroom," I suggested.

"Okay. We can have our dinner there," Geraldine replied.

We headed back to my stateroom.

"What is it?" Geraldine asked.

"I'm sorry to pull you aside like this, but... I need to tell you the truth about my stepfather," I said.

"Okay," she replied.

"My stepfather, Jonathan Conkling, is a very dangerous man, Geraldine. I know this because he poisoned my mother. He was planning to make her seem unwell, mentally. After that, he would commit her to a sanitarium," I said.

"Oh my God. That's awful," Geraldine said. For the first time this whole voyage, I could understand that she was dead serious. She was very emotional.

"Lily, if you need help with anything, I'm here for you. And, I should probably tell you the truth about myself," Geraldine said.

"What is it?" I asked.

"Lily, the truth is... I'm your biological sister," Geraldine said.

My jaw dropped.

"You're my sister?" I asked. I was in awe.

"My true name is Sabrina Ryan," Geraldine said.

"Why the secrecy?" I asked.

She looked at me and said: "You've already met my

superiors, Heinrich Helmfried and Violet Jessop."

"You're a spy?" I asked.

"Yes. Well, actually an undercover agent for the Bureau of Investigation. I'm part of the Bureau of Investigation's Police division," Sabrina admitted.

"But Heinrich works for the Okhrana," I said.

"No. Actually, he *doesn't*," Sabrina responded.

"Tell me why he would keep his true identity a secret. Please," I said.

"When you work in law enforcement, you need a cover, a front, a smokescreen," Sabrina told me.

"So, it was to protect his true allegiance?" I asked.

"Yes. And there's something even more earth-shaking than what I've already told you, Clarissa,"

Sabrina said.

"You mean… Lillian *isn't* my real name?" I asked.

"No. Your full name is Clarissa Lillian Ryan," Sabrina said.

"However," Sabrina began.

"Yes?" I asked.

"That's not the earth-shattering secret," Sabrina said.

"What is it?" I inquired.

"The truth is, Violet Jessop, the head stewardess *and* agent for the Bureau of Investigation, is also your sister. And Heinrich Helmfried? His real name is Henry Ryan. He's your brother," Sabrina said.

"Oh my God," I replied.

"Let me guess. Alyson is also my sister?"

Sabrina nodded.

"She's been working alongside me to take down the three men responsible for Mom's illnesses. I know that we can catch them," Sabrina said.

"I already know who those three are," I confessed.

"You do?" Sabrina asked.

"Yes. Jonathan Conkling, Gunther Zima, and Walter Webb," I said.

I had to understand how Sabrina was my sister.

"Sabrina, are we twins?" I asked.

Sabrina shook her head.

"No. But we are sisters," she answered.

We had to save as many people as we could.

"Clarissa?"

"Yes?" I asked.

"François Fournier is your cousin," Sabrina said.

"Sabrina, I want to be like you. Be able to chase down criminals and make arrests. If it comes to a point where I need to shoot, I'll do it," I said.

Sabrina sighed.

"Clarissa, the job is very dangerous. I don't know how much of it you could handle," Sabrina said.

"Paperwork is just like homework. Not too much different," I said.

"You know something? I'll come with you to the Gymnasium," Sabrina replied.

"Oh, Christ! Is it already that time?" I asked.

"Yes. We better go," Sabrina replied.

We made our way to the Gymnasium.

As we walked into the Gymnasium, I spotted Henry.

He looked us over.

"You're a little bit early," he said.

"No. It's 11:00 right now," Sabrina responded.

"So it is," Henry replied.

"What's the big emergency, Henry?" I asked.

"I hope you brought the notebook with you, Clarissa," he said.

"Why's that?" I asked.

"Do you want there to be hell on Earth?" Henry asked me.

"Of course not!" I said.

"Clarissa, I have it from your sister, Marie Ryan, that you're going to trap the three men responsible for Mother's illnesses and the efforts to render her incompetent. Is this true?" Henry asked.

"You bet your ass it is!" I said.

"How in the Sam Hill do you plan to do that?"

Henry asked.

"Simple. We use Jonathan's own daughter against him. Live bait," I said.

"Oh God. You're bringing the Conkling child into this?" Henry asked.

"Well, what would you do, Einstein?" I asked.

"I would use the notebook as leverage and the necklace too," Henry answered.

"Interesting. How about the other two items that are aboard the ship?" I asked.

"You mean *The Rubaiyat of Omar Khayyam* and *La Circassienne au Bain*?" Henry asked.

"Yes. We know that Jonathan and Gunther both appreciate rare items. Gunther's an art dealer, after all," I said.

Henry chuckled in disbelief.

"Clarissa, do you know exactly where that money goes to?" Henry asked.

"You told me that Gunther is a member of The Black Hand. I heard about them when I was at Sacred Heart Institute!" I said to Henry.

"That's right. The money that Gunther makes from his fraudulent actions is funneled to his terroristic organization," Henry said.

"That's why you've been so observant lately," I said.

"That's right. That's also why I took the alias Heinrich Helmfried.

Your sisters each had to take a different alias as well.

Marie took on the name Violet Jessop and posed as the head stewardess.

Sabrina boarded the ship under the name Geraldine McWright.

However, we've also got our eyes on Melanie McWright," Henry said.

"Why is that?" I asked.

"Do you remember when Gunther said that he pays no attention whatsoever to Serbian affairs?" Sabrina asked me.

"Yes. But, when Max mentioned the annexation of Bosnia, Gunther's eyes flared up with anger. An anger that I never wanted to see," I said.

"You see, Gunther wasn't exactly honest at dinner when he mentioned his mother and her people," Sabrina replied.

"Well, that makes a lot of sense. The son-of-a-bitch is a crook. Of course he'd lie," I said.

I thought about everything that I'd heard.

"At least the second plan worked. Everybody now suspects

*that she's mentally unstable." "Sofia Conkling is unwell.
She's going to be committed to a sanitarium soon."
"What a poor thing."*

All of the things that I'd heard about Mother were
now starting to make sense.

"You don't know the whole truth yet, Clarissa.
Back in the day, Gunther's mother, Marian, was a
well-known art dealer. She also experimented with
jewels. The necklace that Mom currently wears was
made by Marian. Also, she was the most legitimate
jeweler around. However, Gunther didn't care
much for his mother's legitimacy. So, he formed an
organization and had her murdered. In an effort to
cover up his crime, he blamed the Bosnian
annexation. Passionate? Nothing but bullshit! He's
only passionate about materialistic things. Humph.
Slavic trait, my ass. He's a trained assassin," Sabrina
said.

"Stupid militants. They think they can weasel their
way onto a pure ship and force us to give up
everything of great value? I don't think so!" I said in
reply.

"Henry, go to the Cargo Hold. Secure the *Rubaiyat*
and *La Circassienne au Bain.*

Leave them with the Purser," Sabrina ordered.

"Then, let's go back to our cabins. Time is getting on. And Sabrina, you're staying with me tonight," I said.

"Sounds like a good idea to me!" Sabrina replied cheerfully.

"Sabrina, I have something to tend to. I'll catch up with you in a little bit," I said.

"Okay. I'll be waiting for you," Sabrina answered.

I headed to the A-Deck Promenade.

I noticed a woman standing alone.

"Mother? It's freezing! What are you doing out here?" I asked her.

"I can't show my face around there again, Lily. Jonathan lured me out here under the pretense of going for a walk. But, I better tell you the truth anyway. No use in hiding it anymore," she said.

"What do you mean by the truth?" I asked.

"Jonathan received a telegram from his lawyers. He threatened to sell off our estate unless I give him a divorce!" she answered.

"That repugnant son-of-a-bitch! When I get my hands on him, I'll kill him!" I said.

"Whoa! Take it easy, Lily!" Mother exclaimed.

I knew that I had to be calm when speaking to Mother.

"I can't go about taking it easy anymore," I said calmly.

"Why not, sweetheart?"

"Because, when I told Jonathan about the bad steel, I called him an idiot and he told me to take it easy. I hate him!" I replied.

"I hate him too because he stole my necklace!" Mother said.

"When I get through with that stupid, pig-headed, scum-sucking jackass, he'll be dead!" I told her.

"You know, you should be ready for any judgement that'll be cast upon you. For it is written in the gospel of John chapter 8, verse number 7..." Mother began.

"Let him who is without sin among you be the first to cast a stone at her. I know," I said.

"You know that I'm still broken up over my necklace, right?" she said.

"Mother, do you know what I have in my possession at this moment?" I asked.

"Is it what I think it is?" Mother asked.

"Is this what you're looking for?" I asked as I held up

the necklace.

"Oh my God! How did you get it?" Mother asked.

"You would not believe what I've been through tonight!" I answered.

"How do you mean?" Mother asked.

"I mean that I had to go to Gunther's cabin to retrieve it!" I answered.

"Let's talk more about it later," Mother said.

"Okay. Remember: Stay away from Jonathan," I told her.

"All right," she said.

With that, I headed back inside.

"I'll talk to you tomorrow, Mother. I must retire for the night," I said.

"Good night, Mother."

"Good night, sweetheart. I love you," she said.

As I headed back to the stateroom, I couldn't help but think how pleasing it was to have my real family onboard the *Titanic* with me.

"Good night, Sabrina," I said.

Sabrina yawned.

"Good night, Clarissa. I'll talk to you in the morning," she said.

All night long, questions burned in my mind.

If Sabrina and Henry and Alyson and Violet were my real siblings, what did that make Katie?

What did that make Bella?

Was the *Titanic* really in danger?

My concern for Alyson was legitimate and now I knew the reason why.

Jonathan Conkling was Gunther's brother.

The two men were militants for The Black Hand.

I tried my best to go to sleep.

Unfortunately, I couldn't get to sleep.

I was lying wide awake when the sun rose the next morning.

It wouldn't be easy to take down Jonathan, Walter, and Gunther.

I knew that much. But one thing was for damn sure.

The Ryans would never back down from a fight.

The next day, we would strike.

Nine

The decks of the *Titanic* were quiet on Sunday
morning. Everyone had taken to the chapel.

Captain Smith, White Star's most renowned
officer, led the service with an old Naval hymn.

Eternal Father, strong to save,
whose arm hath bound the restless wave,
who bade the mighty ocean deep
its own appointed limits keep:
oh hear us when we cry to thee
for those in peril on the sea.

O Christ, whose voice the waters heard
and hushed their raging at thy word,
who walked upon the foaming deep
and calm amid the storm did sleep:
oh hear us when we cry to thee
for those in peril on the sea.

O Holy Spirit, who did brood
upon the waters dark and rude,
and bade their angry tumult cease,

and gave, for wild confusion, peace:
oh hear us when we cry to thee
for those in peril on the sea.

O Trinity of love and power,
our kindred shield in danger's hour;
from rock and tempest, fire and foe,
protect them wheresoe'er they go;
then evermore shall rise to thee
glad hymns of praise from land and sea.

The hymn was called Eternal Father, Strong to Save.

The song was a ritual for sailors.

Naval sailors or not, the song was vibrant.

However, not all of us attended Sunday services.

Sabrina, myself, Henry, and Marie, stayed out of the public eye.

Now that I knew my true identity, I had to wonder:

How were we supposed to stop Jonathan, Walter, and Gunther without revealing too much?

The question raced in my mind.

I knew that if I wanted to be part of the Bureau Of Investigation's Police division, I needed to prove myself.

"Okay. How do we go about this?" I asked.

"Well, we know that Jonathan, Walter, and Gunther won't stop until we either catch them or kill them or they kill us," Marie said.

"Tell me something that I don't already know!" I said.

"Then you come up with a plan!" Marie shouted at me.

"Keep your tail between your legs, you dog!" I said to Marie.

"Hey! Enough bickering! Marie! Shut up! Clarissa, what's our plan?" Sabrina asked.

"Okay. The way I see it, we use Katie as bait. But, she's not the only bait we have! Behold! The notebook and the necklace!" I said.

"Holy Mother of God!" Sabrina exclaimed as her jaw dropped wide open.

"So, what exactly are we going to do with these items?" Marie asked.

Sabrina turned to Marie, slugged her, and said: "You idiot! We're going to use them as bait!"

"Oh!" Marie said.

"Where exactly do you need us to lure them to?"

Sabrina asked.

"Lure them to the Turkish Bath. Lock them into the Electric Bath," I said.

"Do I have cotton in my ears or did I just hear you say to lock them in the Electric Bath?" Marie asked.

"You heard me, damn it!" I said.

"What's the next part of the plan, genius?" Marie asked.

"Interrogate them," I answered.

"Why are we bringing the Conkling child into this?" a voice asked.

I turned around.

It was Henry.

"I trust you were able to gather the other two items necessary?" I asked.

"Yes. They're with the Purser," Henry replied.

"Good. I don't want those ending up in Jonathan's hands or Gunther's or Walter's!" I said.

"Now, answer me. Why are we bringing the Conkling girl into this?" Henry demanded.

"Someone has to be held for a ransom demand," I answered.

"So, you're going to kidnap her and force Jonathan to react?" Henry asked.

I smirked.

"Yes, Henry!" I replied.

"What if Jonathan catches you doing it, though?" Marie asked.

"Look. We have a code word that we'll use if something goes wrong," I said.

"What is it?" Sabrina asked.

I motioned for Sabrina to come closer.

"What is it?" she asked.

"Give me a Bible," I said.

"Okay," Sabrina replied.

She handed me a Bible.

"Where is it? Where is it? Where is it?" I muttered.

I flipped all the way to the Book of Revelation.

I opened up Revelation 21.

I pointed to Revelation 21:2.

"Read that out loud," I said.

"Okay," Marie replied.

"I saw the holy city, the new Jerusalem, coming down out of Heaven from God, having been prepared as a bride adorned for her husband."

"What are you getting at?" Sabrina asked.

"We'll need three code words," I said.

"Okay. How about: city, Jerusalem, husband?" Marie suggested.

"Perfect!" I said.

"But which word will be the code word for which person?" Marie asked.

"It's very simple," I answered her.

"Let me see if I can figure out," Marie said.

"Okay," I replied.

"City for Webb. Jerusalem for Gunther. Husband for Jonathan," Marie said.

"Yes," I said.

"Clarissa! Here! Catch!" Sabrina said.

She tossed me a handheld device. It looked like something out of a silent film.

"What is this?" I asked.

"It's a CB Radio," Sabrina answered.

She showed me her duty belt equipped with a gun, a pair of handcuffs, and a CB Radio.

"How do I get one of those belts?" I asked.

"Prove yourself and I'll give you a belt with all the equipment necessary," Marie said.

"All right! Sounds good!" I said.

Soon after I had agreed, I heard someone else knock on the door.

"Clarissa? Are you okay in there?" the voice asked.

"Open the door," I said.

The voice opened the door.

It was Alyson.

"Oh! Hi, Alyson!" I remarked.

"Are you okay?" Alyson asked.

"I am now! Thanks!" I said.

"I suppose they didn't tell you my real name, did they?" Alyson asked.

"Wait! You mean your name *isn't* really Alyson?" I asked.

"No. It's not. My real name is Ashley Elizabeth Ryan," she said.

I shot a look at the other three.

"What?!" they all responded.

"You mean to tell me that you didn't bother to let me know who she truly was?" I asked.

"We would have if you had asked," Henry said.

"God damn it, Henry! I *did* ask!" I snapped back.

"Okay! Jesus Christ! Take it easy!" Henry said in reply.

"I will *not* take it easy! I'm sick of people telling me to 'take it easy.' Done!" I said.

"What in God's name has gotten into you, Clarissa?" Marie asked.

"Trust me. If I told you, then you probably

wouldn't believe me!" I said.

"Try me," Marie replied.

I sighed.

"Okay. Here's what happened: I went up to the Smoking Room to talk to Jonathan about getting his precious letter back. I told him he was a fucking idiot. He told me to take it easy," I told her.

"There must be a reason that you got so enraged, Clarissa!" Marie said.

My eyes flared up with a fire that none of them had ever seen.

"Yes. But only myself and Ashley know the reason," I said.

"What is it?" Sabrina asked.

"Ashley?" I said.

Ashley sighed. Her thick Irish accent was gone.

"The Great Lakes Steel Company has been supplying steel for ships. Including for the *Titanic*. Unfortunately, the steel's no good. Great Lakes Steel knew this and gave it to Harland & Wolff to build the *Olympic*, *Titanic*, and what they plan to name *Gigantic*," Ashley said.

Everyone except for myself and Ashley gasped.

Then, Ashley turned to me.

"How did *you* know about it when you didn't even see the contents of the letter?" Ashley asked.

"Another thing that I'm not sure anyone here would believe if I said it," I answered.

Ashley scoffed. "Try me. I believe pretty much anything," she said.

"Fine. Do you know Max Kellermann?" I asked.

Sabrina nodded. Marie nodded. Henry nodded. Ashley shook her head.

"Max works as a buyer for a department store in Brooklyn," I said. "A place called Martin's."

"Okay. How does that have anything to do with the letter?" Ashley asked.

"Well, after Jonathan had sent me to retrieve the letter from you, I had a feeling that it contained information that he wouldn't want getting out," I said.

"So, you told Kellermann about this?" Ashley asked.

"I had to. I didn't have anywhere else to turn at that time," I admitted.

"Well, at least you got it from a trusted source. That's the important thing," Sabrina said.

"Trusted source? What are you talking about? Is Max part of the Bureau of Investigation too?" I asked.

Sabrina shook her head.

"Max is an informant. A consultant, actually. He's helped us out on many cases in the past," Marie answered.

"So, you're telling me that I met with a consultant without knowing?" I asked.

"Well... yes," Ashley said.

"Marie, I have a question for you. I need an honest answer," I said.

"What is it?" Marie asked.

"How consistent are you with a gun?" I asked.

"I'd say I'm the most accurate sharpshooter since Annie Oakley!" Marie boasted.

Sabrina shot her a look that would kill her if looks could kill.

"Boasting never helped anyone, Marie!" she said.

Sabrina's demeanor toward her definitely had put Marie on ice.

"Well, I better go keep an eye out for those three. I don't want them getting past us!" I said.

"You're absolutely right, Clarissa!" Sabrina replied.

I walked out of the first-class cabin.

I kept myself concealed.

Thankfully, I could still see who could be coming.

Just then, I heard laughter.

I turned on the CB radio.

"City, Jerusalem, and husband approaching!" I reported.

"Shit!" Sabrina said.

I got back to base as quick as I could.

"Well, what do we do now?" Ashley asked.

"We've got code words. But we don't have code names yet," I said.

"So, you're saying that we need to come up with code names?" Marie asked.

"Of course that's what I'm saying!" I replied.

"Great! So, how do we come up with them?" Ashley asked.

"Give me the Bible again and I'll figure something out," I answered.

Marie rolled her eyes.

"Damn it, Marie! Don't you dare roll your eyes at her again!" Ashley said as she slugged Marie.

"Well, what is it with her and the damn book?" Marie asked as she handed me the Bible.

"First of all, watch what you say, Marie. Second, the Bible is the most important book to any religious human being!" Sabrina said.

"Yes, ma'am. Sorry, ma'am. I won't do that anymore," Marie apologized.

"That's better. Now, let Clarissa find what she needs to find," Ashley said.

As I was looking for the code names, I heard a knock at the door.

"Would someone answer the damn door?" I asked.

"Got it," Marie said.

She opened the door.

It was Bella.

"Come on in, Bella. Make yourself at home," Ashley said.

"Thank you, Ashley. I'm actually here because I

have been given strict orders to be here," Bella replied.

"Bella, I think you should tell Clarissa your full name," Sabrina said.

I set the Bible down gently.

"Your name *isn't* really Bella, is it?" I asked.

"No. It's not. It's actually Catherine Abigail Ryan," she said.

"Bureau of Investigation?" I asked.

She nodded.

"Great! I figured that something seemed odd at first," I admitted.

Catherine laughed.

"Oh, Clarissa. You're funny!" Catherine said.

"So, tell me. What exactly are you doing? What are you working on?"

"Catherine, I'm trying to come up with code names here for us. Today, we're going to take down the three men responsible for crimes aboard the *Titanic*. I need your help," I replied.

"Okay. Can I see the Bible, please?" Catherine asked.

It was evident that her accent had been phony.

"Sure. Here you go," I said.

I handed her another Bible.

I knew that we would need to work together and piece together all the information that we had.

"Catherine, do you have a pen and some paper?" I asked.

"I do," she said.

She handed me the pen and a full pad of paper.

"Where did you get it?" I asked inquisitively.

"I always keep a pen on me. I got the pad of paper from our mother," Catherine replied.

I wrote down each name I found in the Bible.

The names that I wrote down were:

Anna
Sarah
Martha

Claudia

Candace

Isaiah

I cut out each name.

I handed everyone their code name.

"Sabrina, your code name will be Sarah. Only

respond if I say it," I replied.

"Yes, ma'am. I'll do that," she said.

"Marie. For your code name, I chose Martha. If you hear your code name over the CB radio, respond immediately!" I said.

"Ma'am! Yes, ma'am!" Marie replied, graciously taking her code name slip with her.

"Ashley. For your name, I chose Anna. I needed it to be similar enough to your real name, so that's what I could find. You know the drill," I said.

"Right. Thanks, Clarissa!" Ashley said, giving me a hug.

"Catherine. Your code name is Candace. Only answer your CB radio if I say Candace," I instructed her.

"Yes, ma'am!" Catherine replied.

"Henry. For your name, I had to use Isaiah. There wasn't anything close enough to your first name in the Bible," I said.

"That's all right," he said.

"And Henry, the only time you're allowed to use your code name is if I call up your CB radio," I said.

"Yes, ma'am!" Henry said.

I stuck my code name, Claudia, in my pocket.

"Which name did you pick for yourself, Clarissa?" Ashley asked me.

I pulled out the slip of paper.

"There's my code name!" I said.

"Claudia? Nice pick! It's bordering on your true identity!" Ashley replied.

"Heh. Thanks!" I said with a chuckle.

I knew that we were going to have to get rid of Jonathan, Gunther, and Walter. But how?

"You know something?" I asked Sabrina.

"What's up?" Sabrina asked.

"Maybe we shouldn't arrest them quite yet. We still have to catch them in the act," I said.

"You make a very convincing argument," Sabrina replied.

We decided against arresting the three men. For now, at least.

I went about my daily business.

But, something troubled me. Now that I was about to become an agent with the Bureau Of Investigation, how would I explain it all to Mother?

I kept my eyes open for anything suspicious.

I kept listening for anything suspicious as well.

It wasn't until dinnertime that I overheard something disturbing.

"You know something, gentlemen? When we get to New York, I will have Gunther here send a message back to the Fatherland," Jonathan said.

"Meanwhile, I'll sell the necklace. Sofia won't even suspect a thing!"

I knew at that moment, we were in for one hell of a night.

"Not on my watch, you filthy flea-riddled mongrel mutt!" I thought.

I looked at the three men as they contemplated their next move.

"Of course you will, Jonathan! Let me get the necklace out of my safe!" Gunther said.

"Of course, I'm also going to rally the Bolsheviks!"

"And as a little bit of insurance," Jonathan began.

He flashed his gun.

"Holy shit! What caliber is that?" Gunther asked.

"This is a .45 caliber, my good man. It can vanquish whoever I wish!" Jonathan answered.

The gun had a loaded magazine in it.

I knew that I couldn't let them get to Mother.

It was now evident that Mother had been stashed elsewhere.

It was almost time for us to retire for the night.

Unfortunately, we had a problem. If what François had told us had been the truth, we were going to have a date with destiny. Tonight.

The *Titanic* had been able to dodge icebergs all day.

I looked at my pocket watch.

The time was 11:18 PM.

I rushed to find Sabrina, Catherine, Marie, Ashley, and Henry.

"Sabrina! Where are you?" I called.

I turned on my CB radio.

"Claudia to Sarah. Claudia to Sarah. Do you read me? Over?" I asked.

Suddenly, the CB crackled to life.

"Sarah to Claudia. I read you," Sabrina said.

"What's your 20? Over?" I asked.

"Currently in your cabin," Sabrina answered.

"Okay. I'll be right there!" I replied.

I made my way back to my stateroom.

By the time I got there, it was 11:25 PM.

I turned to Marie.

"Marie, listen to me. I need you to warn Captain Smith," I said.

"Warn him about what?" Marie asked.

I pulled out my pocket watch.

"Look at the time," I said.

"Well, Captain Smith has retired for the evening. Murdoch's in charge now," Marie replied.

"Then, warn Murdoch!" I ordered her.

"Okay. Let me see what I can do," she said.

Marie made her way to the Boat Deck and onto

the Bridge.

"Officer Murdoch! Officer Murdoch!" Marie said.

"What? What? What? What is it, miss?" Murdoch asked.

"I know I'm going to sound crazy, but I need you to take what I'm about to say very seriously. Please," Marie said.

"Very well," Murdoch replied.

"Sir, in a few moments, you're going to receive an attempt at an iceberg warning from the *Californian*. This may be your only chance to save *Titanic* from certain doom," said Marie.

"Well, what do you suggest I do, young lady? Change course?" Murdoch asked.

"Yes. And for the love of God, please do not let the firemen light the last boilers," Marie answered.

"Can't believe I'm taking orders from a passenger," Murdoch muttered under his breath.

"What was that?" Marie asked.

"Nothing. Nothing at all," Murdoch said.

Unfortunately, her pleas came too late.

It wouldn't be long now.

Meanwhile, I had snuck back down to Third-Class.

"Liam! Liam! Where are you?!" I called.

"I'm right here, lass!" he answered.

"Liam, I'm so glad that I found you," I said.

Just then, there was a terrible grinding sound. It was like somebody had scratched their nails on a chalkboard.

"I say, why have we stopped?" a young passenger asked.

"Christ almighty wonder! That was an iceberg!" Liam said.

I figured it was time to tell him the truth.

I looked at him and sighed.

"Liam," I siad.

"Yes?" he asked.

"I haven't been entirely honest with you this whole voyage and I'm sorry about that," I said.

"It's okay, my dear. I understand," he said.

"My real name isn't Lillian," I confessed.

"What *is* your real name?" Liam asked.

"My full name is Clarissa Lillian Ryan," I answered him honestly.

"I'm glad to hear that, because I don't know how much more of that Conkling arsehole I can take!" Liam said with a chuckle.

"Yeah! You and me both!" I said with a laugh.

"Well, I want you to be strong. Promise me that you'll be strong for me," Liam said.

"Liam, if I wanted to go soft, I would've gone soft years ago. I'm harder than a boulder!" I said.

"Until we meet again, Clarissa. I love you," Liam said.

"Liam, come up to the Boat Deck with me," I replied.

"I can't," he said.

I knew that in order to give Liam a fighting chance to get off the *Titanic* alive, I had to be in the worst kind of danger possible.

"Liam, I'm going to rescue my mother. Please, come with me. I need your help," I said.

"Okay," he replied.

We made our way to Gunther's room.

Cabin C-73.

"This is Gunther Zima's cabin," I told him.

I walked quietly to the door and listened.

"Well, Sofia. If I don't leave right now, I'll miss my lifeboat," I heard Gunther say.

I turned to Liam.

"Liam, listen to me. Wait for me in another cabin, okay? I need to do something," I said.

He nodded and spoke not a word.

I turned on my CB radio.

"Claudia to Sarah. Come in, Sarah. Do you read me? Over?" I asked.

Suddenly, my CB radio crackled to life.

"Sarah to Claudia. I read you," Sabrina answered.

"Code word 'murder' is now in effect," I said.

Sabrina rushed to my side.

"Good job calling me up!" Sabrina whispered to me.

"Such a shame, Sofia, that you'll miss the lifeboat unless you tell me where my prized possession is!" Gunther said.

"I already told you! I don't know!" Mother hollered at him.

"Hmm… Then perhaps you'd like to tell me where your thieving bilge rat of a daughter is!" Gunther said.

I kicked in the door and entered.

"I'm right here, you terroristic son-of-a-bitch!" I announced.

"What the fucking hell are you doing here?   And where in the hell is my notebook?!" Gunther demanded.

"What notebook?" I asked.

"Don't play games with me, Lily. My notebook has gone missing. Now, either you have it or the German has it! You'd better tell me who has it!" Gunther said.

He rolled up the sleeve of the cardigan to reveal three words written in capital letters.

On his arm were the words: Unification or Death!

"Wait a second!" I said.

"Ugh. What is it?" Gunther asked, rather annoyed by now.

He was aiming his loaded handgun right at me.

"I know that name! It's another name for The Black Hand!" I said. I was trying to stall for time.

"How right you are, you abomination!" Gunther said.

Gunther kept his gun trained on me.

"Let her go, Gunther! She had nothing to do with your hatred towards me!" I said.

"Hmph. So what? I'm not letting her go! No! I'd like her to see her own daughter getting tortured by me!" he replied maniacally.

"How much crazier can you get?" I asked Gunther.

"I'M NOT CRAZY!!!!!!" Gunther screamed.

"Right. Then, why are you waving a peashooter around when I've got a real gun trained on you already?" I asked.

"You're bluffing, Lily! I'll kill you! Prepare to die at the hands of Serbia!" Gunther said.

"Go ahead and kill me if you dare!" I said.

Gunther aimed his gun at me.

Sabrina burst into the room.

"Gunther Zima! You're under arrest!" Sabrina said.

"Don't try it, you pig!" Gunther said to her.

"Shut up! For the love of God! Shut up, you fucking Serbian son-of-a-bitch!" Sabrina said.

Suddenly, he aimed his gun at her.

"Prepare to die at the hands of Serbia!" Gunther said as he closed in on Sabrina.

She raised her weapon, took aim, and shot him square in the heart.

"Nice shooting!" I said.

"Clarissa, go untie Mom! Now!" Sabrina said.

"Mother? Are you okay now?" I asked.

"Yes! Thanks to you! Both of you!" she said.

Sabrina looked up at her.

"I'm sorry that I wasn't there when you needed me the most, Mom. I wish I would've been," she said.

"Sabrina, it's okay. I knew that you were trying to protect me from Jonathan. That's the reason that you decided to live next door to us!" Mother said.

"Wait a second! You knew?" I asked Mother.

"But of course I did! It wasn't easy to tell Sabrina this, but I needed her onboard the *Titanic*. So, when Jonathan announced that everyone was going to be returning to Minnesota on the *Titanic*, I knew that I had already set a chain reaction in motion. I was going to have Sabrina come with us onboard a different ship. But, the truth is that I hold this one in higher and great regard than I do *Olympic*. Jonathan poisoned me in London. But, he didn't poison me here. Instead, there were two others who poisoned me here. Webb and Gunther," she said.

"Of course!" I said, snapping my fingers.

"What? What is it?" Sabrina asked.

"When an agent boards the *Titanic*, they're given a contact onboard the ship. It just so happened Mom was mine and Henry was yours and Ashley was Catherine's and Catherine was Marie's and Marie was yours," I said.

"So, the poisoning… you intentionally let it happen, Mom?" Sabrina asked.

"Unfortunately, I did. But now, those who don't make it to the boats won't be able to leave on the boats! And Jonathan and Webb are finally getting what they deserve!" Mother said.

"Don't you get it, Sabrina?" I asked.

"Get what?" Sabrina asked.

"Mom was deep undercover. She had to make sure

that she knew the man she was going to arrest would be capable of such a crime! She needed Jonathan to poison her in London and then have Webb poison her one night on here and then have Gunther do the same!" I said.

"Wow! Unbelievable! I can't believe how much hard work you put into this, Mom!" Sabrina remarked.

Mother laughed.

"Well, I was quite something before I had you. But, I guess I still *am* something!" she said.

"Everyone! Get your lifebelts on! Right now!" I heard a voice holler from outside the cabin.

I opened the door.

It was the real Violet Jessop. The same one who had greeted us days earlier.

"Not a moment to lose, Miss Clarissa!" Violet said.

"Violet! I need you to do something for me!" I replied.

"What is it?" she asked.

"I need you to escort my mother and my sister up to the Boat Deck! I'll be up in a little bit! I need to do something first!" I said.

"Right. Come along, ladies!" Violet replied.

I put on my lifebelt and then found Liam.

He was in C-59.

"Liam! Hurry! We need to go!" I said.

"Okay! I'm downright ready, I am!" Liam replied.

"Look. Liam, you need to get up on the Boat Deck! Right now! I've got a few more folks to get off the ship!" I said.

"Okay! Promise me that you'll get up there when you can!" Liam said.

"I promise!" I said.

Liam rushed up to the Boat Deck.

I grabbed Gunther's knife.

I stuck it in my pocket.

I turned on my CB radio.

"Claudia to Isaiah. Do you read me? Over?" I asked.

"Copy that. I read you," Henry answered.

"Hurry and get to the Boat Deck! I'll meet you there! Over!" I said.

"Okay. I'll see you up there!" Henry answered.

"Claudia to Candace. Come in, Candace. Do you read me? Over?" I asked.

"Candace to Claudia. I read you," Catherine answered.

"Get your lifebelt on! Meet me on the Boat Deck!" I said.

"Whose orders were those?" Catherine asked.

"Captain Smith! Who else?" I responded.

"All right. I'll head up right now!" Catherine said.

"Claudia to Anna. Come in, Anna. Do you read me? Over?" I asked.

"Anna to Claudia. Copy that," Ashley answered.

"Get your lifebelt on and get up to the Boat Deck! It's the Captain's orders!" I said.

"Promise me that you'll be careful?" Ashley asked.

"Of course, I'll be careful!" I said.

"Claudia to Martha. Come in, Martha. Do you copy? Over?" I asked.

"Martha to Claudia. I read you. What's the situation?" Marie asked.

"We struck an iceberg and we're sinking by the bow. Get your lifebelt on and get up on the Boat Deck!" I said.

"All right! Just promise me that you'll be there!" Marie answered.

"I promise you! I'll be there!" I replied.

"Great!" Marie said.

"Now, I've got one more person to take to the Boat Deck!" I said.

"Okay! I'll see you up there!" Marie said.

I turned off my CB radio.

I headed up to the Boat Deck.

By the time I reached the Boat Deck, the bow was nearly submerged in water.

"And I saw a new Heaven and a new Earth, for the first Heaven and the first Earth had passed away. And there was no more sea. And I saw the holy city, new Jerusalem, coming down out of Heaven from God, prepared as a bride adorned for her husband. And I heard a loud voice from the Throne saying: Behold! The tabernacle of God is among men! And He shall dwell with them. And they shall be His people and God Himself will be with them and be their God. And God will wipe away all tears from their eyes and there shall be no more death. Neither shall there be any more sorrow or crying. Neither shall there be any more pain. For the former things have passed away," I heard a man say.

I looked over just in time to see a young priest.

"My God! That's Father Thomas Byles!" Liam

said.

Just then, I heard a sound like a slingshot or a rubber band breaking. I watched as the first funnel of the great ocean liner crashed into the sea.

"Where's Father Peruschitz?" I asked.

"Peruschitz decided to try his luck back inside. I'm not sure if he knew that we struck an iceberg," Sabrina said.

"Wow. What a brave guy," I said.

Four priests had sailed on the *Titanic*. None of them took a seat in the lifeboat. Father Josef Benedikt Peruschitz, who was a missionary from Germany, was on his way to Minnesota to join the faculty at St. John's Abbey.

Reverend Robert J. Bateman, an English priest, had been married in the United States, and had preached in the United States and lived in the United States. He visited England again in early 1912, but only stayed for a couple months. o

Father Juozas Montvila, a 27-year-old Lithuanian priest, had been forced to leave his homeland under the threat of persecution.

Father Thomas Byles, aged 42, had served Saint Helen's parish in Ongar, Essex, England. Byles had advocated for his parish and parishioners. However, his brother, William, called on him to celebrate his wedding. Byles, a man of God, promised his brother that he would be there. Byles booked passage on the *Titanic* as a Second-Class passenger. Now, the only thing that worried me was the fate that all of the priests would meet.

I looked around.

Finally, I saw Marie.

"Marie!" I said

"Though I walk through the valley of the shadow of death, I shall fear no evil, for thou art with me. Thy rod and thy staff. They comfort me," Byles continued.

"Clarissa! Are you all right?!" Marie asked.

"I'm fine. We don't have much time," I answered.

"You're right. What do you suggest we do?" Marie asked.

"See to it that everyone else is in a lifeboat before you and Liam and myself!" I ordered her.

"But—" Marie began to protest.

"That's an order, Detective!" I replied.

"Okay. Okay. Fine. Fine. Fine. I'll see to it," Marie said.

"We be goin' down. Down to Davy Jones' Locker," I heard a crewman say.

"Davy Jones' Locker? That's the legendary burial place for sailors and mariners lost to the sea or the ocean. No man who has ever set foot in there has ever made it out alive!" I thought. Of course, I knew that it was a place of nautical folklore. I had fancied myself reading *Moby-Dick, or The Whale* by Herman Melville.

"I'm going to see if I can convince Jonathan to come up to the Boat Deck," I said.

I walked into the First Class Lounge.

"You are proving surprisingly hardy!" Jonathan said.

"You're coming with me, whether you like it or not!" I replied.

"The hell I am!" Jonathan snapped at me.

"Do you want to survive the sinking or do you want to try to be a hero?" I asked.

"You can get me off the ship?" Jonathan asked, naturally skeptical.

"Of course I can! I am a girl, after all!" I said.

"I hate when you bring that up," he replied.

"Here. Put this on," I said as I handed him a shawl.

"A shawl?! Good God! I'm a man!" Jonathan said.

"It's your only chance at survival!" I reminded him.

"Fine. Give me the damn shawl!" he said.

I knew that we were going to have to get to the boats and fast!

I made my way to the Boat Deck.

"By the way, Jonathan, I have the letter," I said.

I was clearly bluffing, but Jonathan couldn't tell.

"Give it to me! Give me the letter! Now!" Jonathan shouted.

"You are so stupid! I don't actually have the letter!" I said, laughing.

"Give me the damn letter!" Jonathan demanded.

"You'll see the letter when you're closing down your steel company, dumbass!" I said.

"You bitch! I should kill you right now!" Jonathan snarled.

He rolled up his sleeve to reveal his true identity. A tattoo in black ink of a hand print emerged.

"Too bad I already knew that about you," I said.

"What you don't know *can* kill you! I should've killed you long ago! My name isn't Jonathan Conkling. My name is Arnold Zima! I am a member of The Black Hand! Prepare to die at the hands of Serbia!" he said, snarling at me.

He reached for a gun. Luckily, I noticed Officer Murdoch nearby.

"Mister Murdoch!" I said.

"Yes, miss? What is it?" Murdoch asked.

"Can I borrow your gun for a brief second?" I asked.

"Are you in danger, miss?" Murdoch asked.

Yes. If you consider my stepfather trying to murder me as being in danger, then, yes. I'm in danger," I said.

Fine. Here's the gun. Give it back to me as soon as you're done with it," Murdoch said.

"Thanks! I owe you!" I said.

I took aim at Arnold, squeezed the trigger, and shot him in the heart, killing him instantly.

I blew out the smoke from the gun.

"Here you are, my good man," I said.

"Thank you, Miss," Murdoch replied.

"All part of my job description!" I said.

"What do you mean?" Murdoch asked.

"The truth is, I'm not just any passenger, Mister Murdoch. My name is Clarissa Ryan.
Bureau Of Investigation," I confessed.

"What kind of agent doesn't have her own gun?" Murdoch asked.

"A rookie," I replied, blushing.

"I see. That figures," Officer Murdoch said.

"Officer Murdoch, it's been a pleasure," I said.

I started to walk away.

"Clarissa! Wait! I've got something for you!" Officer Murdoch called to me.

"What is it, Will?" I asked.

"Here. Take this with you," Officer Murdoch answered. He handed me his gun.

"Thank you, sir. But are you sure that you—?" I began to ask.

Aye. Don't worry yourself none. I got meself a spare," Murdoch said, answering my question before the rest of it could escape my lips.

"Officer Murdoch, I will always remember you. I'll remember you and Captain Smith and Mr. Andrews and Chief Officer Wilde and all of the great crew members aboard the *Titanic*. Thank you for your service, kind sir," I said.

"It was… a pleasure," Officer Murdoch replied.

Just then, I saw Reverend Bateman.

"Ada, take this with you and see that Emily gets it," Reverend Bateman said, handing a book to his sister-in-law.

"*Ada must be Ada Balls, Bateman's sister-in-law*," I thought.

"But, Robert, won't you even try to make it?" Ada asked.

"The Lord God has told me that it's my time to come home. I heard Him last night. He came to me in a vision. He told me that someone had made a mockery of Him by saying that He couldn't sink this mighty ocean liner. I have come to accept my fate. It's only fair that Emily gets my Bible. Please. Do this for me, if not for the Lord our God," Bateman said.

By now, I could see Ada's eyes filling up with tears.

Well, at least people are beginning to accept that this ship is not unsinkable and that we're sinking. Sinking by the bow, no less," I thought.

Ten

The *Titanic* was already sinking quickly.

I glanced at my pocket watch.

"*12:10 AM*," I thought.

The *Titanic*, designed to be unsinkable, was about to sink.

Arnold Zima, formerly known as Jonathan Conkling, was lying dead on the Boat Deck.

"Okay. Okay. I'm going. I'm going," he replied.

"*Now, to save three more people*," I thought.

This was going to be a little bit easier since both men were in the Smoking Room.

I burst into the Smoking Room.

"Max! Max! Max!" I called.

"Lily! Thank God!" Max said.

"Max. I need you to listen to me very carefully," I told him.

"Okay. Go on," he replied.

"We've struck an iceberg. Get your lifebelt on and go out to the lifeboats!" I said.

"Okay. Thanks!" he replied.

"François!" I said.

"Ah! My dear cousin! What has been troubling you?" he asked.

"First of all, I know your name isn't really François. It's Francis. Francis Martin," I said.

"You are correct," he replied.

"And second, get your lifebelt on and get out on the Boat Deck! The *Titanic* is going to sink!" I said as I emphasized the importance of the grave situation.

"Way ahead of you, cousin!" Francis replied.

"For God's sakes! Just call me Clarissa!" I snapped at him.

"Fine. Clarissa, let's go!" Francis remarked.

It was crucial that we got everything and everyone that we could get off the ship.

"I'll be right there!" I told Francis.

Francis had finally dropped his ridiculously phony French accent.

He made his way to the Boat Deck.

The grandest ship in the world was about to meet her fate.

I burst into Katie's stateroom.

"Katie! Come on, honey!" I said.

"Lily, is everything okay?" Katie asked.

"Come on! There's not much time left! Let's go! By the way, my name is Clarissa Ryan," I told her.

"Okay. I'm coming, Clarissa," Katie said.

I eventually made my way to the Boat Deck.

I saw Murdoch.

I also saw Lightoller and some of the other officers.

I knew them all by name.

"Officer Pitman, how many boats are left?" I asked.

"A few on the starboard side forward, Miss. Plenty more aft," he answered.

"Officer Pitman, I know you say that you require only women and children at this time, but I have a few people that I need to get back home," I said.

"Young lady, I do hope you're not tryin' to bribe me. That would be illegal," Pitman replied.

"I'm not attempting to bribe you. Don't worry. My name is Clarissa Ryan. I'm with the Bureau Of

Investigation," I told him.

"Then what do you need me to do?" Officer Pitman asked.

"Please let me take my siblings and someone special to me in a lifeboat," I said.

"Oh. All right. Fine," Pitman replied.

"Thank you, Officer Pitman!" I said happily.

"Remember, ma'am: Once you board the lifeboat, you and everyone with you will have to do as the Officer manning the boat tells ya to," Pitman said.

"Of course, Officer Pitman!" I said.

I looked around.

"Catherine! Henry! Sabrina! Ashley! Marie! Katie! Mother!" I said.

"What is it?" Catherine asked.

"I got a lifeboat for all of us!" I said.

"How did you manage that?" Henry asked.

"I just told Officer Pitman that I needed a boat for all of us. He said he'd allow it, but just this once. No exceptions," I said.

"Great! Then, let's do it!" Henry said.

I grabbed Liam.

"Come on," I said.

"Okay. I'm coming!" Liam responded.

"Is this everyone?" Pitman asked.

"Yes," I answered.

"I guess that I'm going to be manning this boat," Pitman said.

I remembered our lifeboat number.

"Can I be of any help?" a voice asked.

It was Max Kellermann.

"Yes. Please do!" Pitman said.

"What can I do to help?" Max asked.

"You see those ropes?" Pitman asked.

  "Yes," Max replied.

"They're called falls. I need you to get someone to cut them," Pitman said.

"All right, Herbert. I will," Max replied.

Max looked around.

 "There's Officer Moody! Get his attention, Max!" I said.

"Officer Moody? Officer Moody!" Max called to him.

"Yes?" Moody replied.

"I need someone to cut the falls. Will you do that?" Max asked.

"Of course I'll do that, son," he said.

"You wouldn't happen to have a knife about you, would ya?"

Max climbed into the boat.

"Clarissa, I need the knife," Max told me.

"Of course, Max! Here!" I said.

I handed him the knife.

"Here you go, Officer Moody," Max said, handing him the knife.

"Thank ya, Mr. Kellermann. I'll give ya back yer knife after I cut these falls," Moody said.

The falls broke and Moody closed up the blade and handed it to Max.

"Thanks!" Max said.

"Best of luck to ya, Kellermann," Moody said.

"Likewise, Officer Moody. Godspeed, sir," Max replied.

"Well, Mr. Kellermann, we have space for one more person," Pitman said.

"You mean I can get in the boat?" Max asked.

"Yes. Max, get in the boat!" I said.

Max climbed into the boat.

I already knew that Francis had made it off the sinking ship.

I saw Bruce Ismay climb into a lifeboat.

"*What a coward*," I thought disgustedly. Murdoch cut the falls.

We watched as the lights flickered. Finally, the lights on the famous liner went out one last time. This time, forever.

I heard a hymn play. I recognized it as Reverend Bateman's favorite song. It was *Nearer, My God To Thee*.

I turned to Max.

"Max, it's time you know my real name. The name Lily Conkling was an alias," I confessed.

"Okay," he said.

"My real name is Clarissa Ryan," I said.

"And then I take it that you've got a brother, wonderful sisters, and a great boyfriend. Not to mention a great mother," Max replied. He wasn't sure if he'd ever find true love, the poor guy.

But, just then, Catherine looked at him.

"Max, will you be my boyfriend?" Catherine

asked.

"Of course, darlin'!" Max said.

I swear to God. His face lit up like a Christmas tree. He was all too giddy.

I turned to Liam.

"You'll love Minnesota!" I said.

Liam chuckled.

"I ain't been out of Europe before, however, 'tis starting to sound more and more enjoyable every time ya talk about it!" Liam said.

The Bible verses from earlier had stuck in my head.

"Hail Mary, full of grace. The Lord is with thee.

Blessed art Thou among women, and blessed is the fruit of Thy womb, Jesus. Holy Mary, Mother of God, pray for us sinners, now and at the hour of our death. Amen," I said.

"Glory be to the Father, and to the Son and to the Holy Spirit. As it was in the beginning, is now, and always shall be, world without end. Amen."

Sabrina looked at me for a little while.

Finally, she asked: "What are you doing, Clarissa?"

I looked her in the eye and said:

"I'm praying. Praying that we'll be saved."

"Can I do it too?" Sabrina asked.

"Sure. Hold my hand and we'll pray together," I said.

Sabrina grasped my hand.

"Our Father who art in Heaven. Hallowed be Thy name. Thy Kingdom come. Thy will be done on Earth as it is in Heaven. Give us this day our daily bread and forgive us our debts as we forgive our debtors. And lead us not into temptation, but deliver us from evil. For Thine is the Kingdom, the Power and the Glory. Forever and ever. Amen," we prayed.

It was 2:19 AM on Monday, April 15, 1912. For a brief minute, the stern of the *Titanic* stayed pointed at the stars.

At 2:20 AM, the great liner slipped beneath the calm North Atlantic Ocean.

"Great Scott! She's gone," Pitman said.

"Oh my goodness! How are we going to tell everyone back home?" I asked.

There were a few more things that I had to arrange before we made our way onto the *Carpathia*, which was the rescue ship commissioned by the Cunard Line.

"Ashley, I want for you, Mom, Sabrina, Catherine, Henry, Marie, Max, and Liam to come and live with me," I said.

"You're kidding!" Sabrina said, shocked.

"I don't kid," I said.

"Oh my goodness! You're serious!" Catherine said.

"That's right! I've never been more serious about a living situation than I am right now!" I said.

After we were onboard the *Carpathia*, I sat down with Liam.

"What do you think?" I asked.

"I think it'll be nice," he said.

"Oh! Mom? I have someone that I grabbed just before we made our way off the *Titanic*," I said.

"What? Who?" she asked.

I turned to Sabrina.

"Sabrina, you might want to let her go see Mom," I said.

"Mommy! Mommy! Mommy!" a tiny voice cried.

I watched Katie run to Mother.

"Katie! How are you, baby?" Mother asked.

"I'm doing good. A little rattled, but I'm glad I'm safe!" Katie said.

"You know something, Mom?" Sabrina asked.

"What's that?" Mother inquired.

"There won't be any wars happening anytime soon!" Marie chimed in.

"That's right!" I said.

"Why exactly is that?" Mother asked.

"Mom, you know the reason. And you know the people who were responsible for stopping these wars from happening! You also know the people who could have started those wars," Sabrina said.

"What do you mean I know the reason?" Mother asked sharply. She was still very cold, so she didn't mean to come across very sharply.

"Come with us," Liam said.

"Very well," she replied.

We made our way to our new stateroom.

"Okay. Sabrina, show her the notebook. Henry, I want you to show her the necklace. Marie, it's your job to make a chart. I'll explain everything," I said.

"Right," they responded.

Marie drew a huge circle.
In each section, she wrote something.

One section was "Profits"

Another section was "The Black Hand."

Another one said "Items to fund The Black Hand."

The next one read: "Items received by The Black Hand."

Another one said: "Items used to thwart the assassination of Archduke Franz Ferdinand."

She carefully wrote out each word.

"All of these items have sentimental value, Mom. If they were to fall into the wrong hands, chaos would ensue. There would be hell on Earth," Marie said.

"Everything has sentimental value except for the notebook. No sentimental value there," I corrected her.

"Okay. Fine. Everything except the notebook has sentimental value," Marie said.

"Why is this notebook so important, anyhow?" Mother asked.

"Mom, this notebook isn't your average notebook. I mean it *was* at one point your average notebook. But this notebook contains valuable classified information," Marie answered her.

"This information could *ruin* Serbia," I said, emphasizing the importance.

"Clarissa! Shhh!" Marie replied.

"Marie, I proved myself this past evening.

The Lord God knows I'm not going into the steel industry," I said.

"Damn right!" Sabrina piped up.

"Mother, I'd like to join Sabrina and Henry and Marie and Ashley and Catherine as part of the Bureau Of Investigation. Please," I said.

"It's fine with me as long as it's okay with them," she said.

"Welcome to the Bureau Of Investigation, Clarissa!" Ashley said.

I looked at my hands. I still had the gun Murdoch had given me.

I turned to Liam.

"You know that I'll always be home after work, right?" I said.

"Of course I know that, honey. I love you," he said.

We returned to Minnesota, and moved to a small township of 424 people in central Minnesota.

It was called Miltona Township.

We had all seen the ship split in half.

Over 1500 people died that night.

But, thankfully, we survived. Arnold Zima, otherwise known as Jonathan Conkling, was dead.

The final White Star Line ocean liner was named *Britannic*. She sailed from 1916 until 2012.

Soon after the *Titanic* disaster, new safety laws were instigated.

The World Wars never occurred. Neither did the Korean War, the Cold War, or even the attack on America's most famous structure: The World Trade Center in New York.

In July of 1915, a Great Lakes liner named the *Eastland* capsized, killing 844 people. The *S.S. Eastland* was moored when she capsized.

Unlike the ships who preceded her, *Eastland* was built for speed, not stability.

In 1927, Dr. Robert Goddard, a scientist, got America involved in another frontier that would become known as The Last Frontier.

That was Spaceflight. Missions to the Moon, Mars, and more.

42 years after Goddard's rocket, and 8 years after Yuri Gagarin became the first man in space, the Americans were still behind the Soviets. But, thanks to the genius mind of Wernher von Braun, the Americans would win the Space Race.

Catherine and Max married on April 15, 1922. They had five children.

In 1972, Catherine retired from the FBI. She established an academy for children who wanted to become FBI agents.

She passed away 40 years later.

Max followed shortly after.

Marie eventually retired from her position in the FBI. She went on to establish the Marie Ryan Foundation. She sent the letter about Great Lakes Steel to a newspaper in Duluth shortly after the return to Minnesota. At that point, Marie, Catherine, Henry, Ashley, and myself, raided the steel mill.

Ashley retired from the FBI in 1966. She became an author and wrote the novel *Titanic A Ship Out Of Time*. She married her husband, Michael, in 1969.

Henry married his high school sweetheart, Donna, in 1913. He retired from the FBI in 1992. They bore five children too.

Sabrina eventually met a young man from the township of Miltona. They were married on April 25, 1912. Eventually, Sabrina retired from the FBI and became a full-time author. Her book, *Sabrina Ryan: Stories of an FBI Agent*, would eventually become a best-seller. Sabrina passed away in 2029. She and her husband bore five children.

I married Liam on May 15, 1912. It was the one month anniversary of the *Titanic* disaster, but I knew Mother's old saying: "An opportunity can crawl under the rug at any moment. Don't let your opportunity dust you off. Grab it before it can slip away. The only opportunity to act may come around once or twice in your life."

We had five more children.

In 2022, 110 years after the *Titanic* disaster, Liam and I breathed our last.

At our funeral, our children and others eulogized us.

Our youngest daughter, Emma Lynn, recited the same Bible verse that Liam and I had heard 110 years earlier on the *Titanic*.

"And I saw a new Heaven and a new Earth, for the first Heaven and the first Earth had passed away. And there was no more sea. And I saw the holy city, new Jerusalem, coming down out of Heaven from God, prepared as a bride beautifully adorned for her husband. And I heard a loud voice from the Throne saying: Behold! The tabernacle of God is among men! And He shall dwell with them. And they shall be His people and God Himself shall be with them and He shall be their God. And God will wipe away all tears from their eyes and there shall be no more death. Neither shall there be any more sorrow or crying. Neither shall there be any more pain. For the former things have passed away," she said. Our daughter, Georgia, had this to say: "When I first talked to Mom and Dad about the *Titanic* disaster, they didn't want to offer me a lot of detail. That's understandable.

But, eventually, they became much more understanding. It was after one of my conversations with my mom that she finally revealed the truth to me. A truth that would change my views of the world before my parents took it upon themselves to depart from the *Titanic*. My mother told me that when she was young, a great evil threatened to destroy the entire world. Corruption was abound at that point. My grandfather wasn't who he claimed he was. My grandfather turned out to be one of the most wanted men in the world. His name was Arnold Zima. He had assumed the name Jonathan Conkling. He married my grandmother, Sofia. But, right away, my mother, my aunts, and my uncle, all knew that something was awfully suspicious about the man my grandmother had married. It wasn't until April 13, 1912, that Mom's worst fears were confirmed. My grandmother had been getting poisoned by my grandfather. But, as sure as I'm standing here today, I can tell you that nothing like that shall ever occur in this world again!

We must stand as pillars of our community!

Pillars of justice! Pillars of freedom! Pillars of truth! Pillars of honesty! Pillars of integrity! Pillars of dignity! Pillars of trust! Pillars of law! Pillars of faith! And pillars of honor! But, most importantly, we must stand as pillars of support! Support not just for ourselves, but for each other! For it is written: "You shall love your neighbor as yourself." Dad was very worried that I wouldn't be able to handle the truth about the ill-fated voyage. Over 1500 people met a watery grave on the morning of April

15, 1912. The horror that my parents must have felt had to be greatly immense. The way Mom described it to me was that it was like David and Goliath with David shooting a pebble at Goliath's head using his slingshot. The breakup of the *Titanic* was much harsher than anyone thought it would be. Imagine 20,000 to 30,000 tons of water pressure on a ship that's got a Gross Register Tonnage of 44,000+ tons. My mother especially loved anything that was of great interest to Americans. It didn't matter if it was a new luxury vehicle, a new fashion trend, or if it had to do with transportation, such as human spaceflight. Looking back on their lives, I can say that my mom loved the space program. Everything from Project Mercury up to the Space Shuttle was important to her."

Everyone else stood up.

"I will stand as a pillar!" they said.

Claris, our middle child, quoted one of America's greatest men: "A house divided against itself cannot stand." The quote was from the late President, Abraham Lincoln, who was assassinated in 1865.

Our son, Willi, had become a minister.

He recited Psalm 23.

The Lord is my shepherd. I shall not want.

He maketh me to lie down in green pastures. He leadeth me beside the still waters.

He restoreth my soul. He leadeth me in the paths of righteousness for His name's sake.

Though I walk through the valley of the shadow of death, I shall fear no evil for Thou art with me. Thy rod and Thy staff. They comfort me.

Our children went on to have their own children. We never met our grandchildren.

They named them after loved ones, such as myself, Liam, Sabrina, Catherine, Marie, Henry, and Ashley.

In 1985, Dr. Robert Ballard, an oceanographer, located the wreck of the *Titanic*. The date was September 1. The time was 2:20 AM.

I closed my eyes that night and remembered hearing the sound of the music. The very tune that was played that echoed across the Atlantic.

It was a hymn called *Nearer My God To Thee*. It was played to the tune of *Bethany*.

Others would argue that the song was *Songe d'Automne*, otherwise called *Autumn Dream*, a song written by Archibald Joyce.

But I knew exactly what I heard that night.

The song was clear. Just like the waters of Lake Miltona.

Alas, a bitter end to what would've been a legendary maiden voyage aboard a legendary ship.

Many lives were cut short.

However, I could still remember the fresh air that filled my lungs after my career in the FBI ended. We had set up an FBI office in Miltona.

In 1975, Great Lakes Steel bid farewell to its workers. The company had a meeting with the wrecking ball. The mill was condemned.

The company, Duluth Hilltop Construction, employed wreckers as well.

The wrecker swung the mighty crane at the foundry. One. Two. Three. I counted off the number of the swings as I had been there to watch the destruction of the foundry that had produced the flawed steel. The steel was absolutely no good. It was used in the *Titanic*, *Olympic*, and *Britannic*. I still remembered having taken strolls along the decks of *Titanic*, *Olympic*, and *Britannic*.

In 1981, the FBI Office in Miltona folded.

With no crimes to solve, I retired from the FBI office in Miltona.

The only case that I ever solved was back in 1912. Back when there was sheer terror and panic. A year that would always be remembered as the year that we had a date with destiny. My mission aboard the *Titanic* was a success. I successfully rooted out the militants of The Black Hand.

In 1898, 14 years before *Titanic*, an author named Morgan Robertson wrote a novella. It was titled

The Wreck of Titan.

The novella may have predicted the *Titanic* disaster years before it occurred. It wasn't until 1912 that I would find out exactly how true that was. Before his death, Robertson denied that he was a psychic. "I only wrote from my experience what I know about ships. I am not a clairvoyant. It was merely a coincidence that the *Titanic* disaster happened exactly as it did to the fictional S.S. *Titan* in my story," Robertson said.

However, I was left wondering: *Was* it truly a coincidence or was there something more to it? An unforeseen power at work? I didn't know.

But, unfortunately, with Robertson's death in 1915, I felt that I might never get my answer. So, I bought an original copy of the novella. I knew that I had to get to the bottom of the mystery. Using my skills to determine if the novella did, in fact, predict the *Titanic* disaster, I came to the most logical conclusion that I could. *Futility; Or the Wreck of Titan*, written by Morgan Robertson, had, in fact, predicted the *Titanic* disaster.

Acknowledgements

My name is Michael Koebnick.

When I was born, I became fascinated with the *Titanic*. It was a mystery to me. This was, without a doubt, one of the most interesting topics in history. Just like everybody's favorite amateur sleuth in fiction, Nancy Drew, I love a good mystery. My love for mysteries gave me the idea for code names and integrating the FBI's predecessor, the Bureau Of Investigation, into my novel. When I was in Kindergarten, I got my first copy of the computer game *Titanic Adventure Out Of Time*.

My characters, as well as the subplots and themes, were based entirely on the game.

When you love something, you never get sick of it. Ever. I completed the game in every possible way. Every time I completed it, I either received a game over or a perfect ending or, even, the optimal ending.

I also want to clarify a few things.

The FBI field office in the township of Miltona is fictious. All of the characters, save for some historical figures, are fictitious.

Duluth Hilltop Construction is fictitious.

The speech that I would like to refer to as The Pillars speech, was a speech that I came up with as a means of support for those who need support. Be true to your fellow man. Follow your brothers and sisters in conquering all injustices. Honor your brother and your sister. Honor your father and your mother. Honor all.

Be ready for anything. Be the voice for the mute. Be the voice of reason. Be the hope for those in despair. Be a beacon of light in a cave of darkness. Be true to yourself. Be willing. Be ready. Be able. Focus your energy on helping each other. The world does not need anymore bloodshed. That is why I based this book on the good ending and the perfect game ending.

The items *The Rubaiyat of Omar Khayyam* and *La Circassienne au Bain* were real items. Both were lost in the sinking of the *Titanic*. The notebook and necklace were fictitious and based on the Lambeth Diamonds from *Titanic Adventure Out of Time*.

In the last chapters of the book, I was inspired by the Book of Revelation in the Holy Bible. Specifically, Chapter 21. Verses 1, 2, 3, and 4. As well as Psalm 23. Verses 1 through 4.
The passages on the *Titanic* and at the funeral are both from the Holy Bible.
 So, my parents bought me books about shipwrecks, and even books related specifically to the *Titanic*. In the year 2018, I bought the Kindle edition of *Titanic: A Ship Out of Time* by Ashley Herzog, formerly Ashley Bristow. I want to thank her for writing such a wonderful book. Ashley, when it comes to historical fiction, you, my friend, are amazing! I drew my inspiration from your novel! You are truly awesome!

You are also a truly wonderful editor!

I also want to thank Cyberflix, the developers of the game. I also want to thank Bill, Todd, and Tom Appleton for their fantastic work on the game, as well as Andrew Nelson. Bill, Tom, and Todd Appleton founded Cyberflix. Tom Appleton portrayed Vlad Demonic in the game *Titanic Adventure Out Of Time*. The game hasn't been physically released since 2001.

I would like to thank Cyberflix for allowing me to be inspired by *Titanic Adventure Out of Time*. Full credits for the game can be found on the Internet Movie Database. Please visit this link for the full writing credits for the game: https://www.imdb.com/title/tt0176236/

When *Titanic Adventure Out of Time* was first released, I learned a lot about history much earlier than one would normally learn.

If you got one of the bad endings, it was evident by the *Memories* book in the game.

Jonathan Conkling, real name Arnold Zima, was based on Andrew Conkling.

Gunther Zima, the sleazy art dealer, was based on Sasha Barbicon and Vlad Demonic.

Sofia Conkling was based on Georgia Lambeth.

Lily Conkling, real name Clarissa Ryan, was based on Frank Carlson.

Sabrina Ryan, alias Geraldine McWright, was based on Claris Limehouse.

Ashley Ryan, alias Alyson Haynes, was based on Shailagh Hacker.

Liam Haynes was based on Jack Hacker.

Henry Ryan, alias Heinrich Helmfried, was based on Willi von Haderlitz.

Catherine Ryan, alias Bella, was based on Daisy Cashmore.

Marie Ryan, alias Violet Jessop, was based on Penny Pringle and Steward Smethells.

Melanie McWright was based on Mrs. Limehouse.

Francis Martin, alias François Fournier, was based on Buick Riviera.

Max Kellermann was based on Max Seidelmann.

Other characters in the book were based on other characters from the game.

Characters in the book who either appeared or were mentioned and were historical figures include:

Violet Jessop

Captain Edward John Smith

First Officer William Murdoch

Second Officer Charles Lightoller

Third Officer Herbert Pitman

Fourth Officer Joseph Boxhall

Fifth Officer Harold Lowe

Sixth Officer James Moody

Chief Officer Henry Wilde

Father Thomas Byles

Reverend Robert J. Bateman

Father Josef Peruschitz

Morgan Robertson

Father Juozas Montvila

Robert Ballard

Other historical figures who were mentioned in the book, yet had no connection to the *Titanic* disaster, included:
Robert Goddard
Wernher von Braun

The book was very interesting to write, but at the same time, it was very heart-breaking.

There are more books about Clarissa and her family to come.

I figure that I should separate fiction and reality.

In the book, neither *Lusitania* or *Britannic* sink.
Therefore, the World Wars are averted.
However, in reality, World War I and World War
II both occurred. Also, the *Lusitania* and *Britannic*
did sink in reality. It was due to the sinking of the
Lusitania that the United States, the Allied Forces,
entered World War I.

This was not easy for me to write because I didn't
want to blur the lines of reality and fiction. I
understand how hard it is for some people to keep
them separated. For me, I learned it early in life.

I took the subplots of *Titanic Adventure Out Of
Time* and got creative with them. In doing so, I
corrected an error that is in the game. When you're
searching for the painting, it's not a painting that
would've been available until 1914.

In addition, I decided to include The Lord's Prayer,
also called the Our Father, in this book because I
felt that most of the passengers were praying to be
rescued. Praying to survive the frigid waters of the
North Atlantic Ocean. Praying for, as it was quoted
in the movie, *Titanic*, "an absolution that would
never come."

Printed in Great Britain
by Amazon

52074058R00122